The Jack of Hearts

A Murder Mystery

By

P C Brooke

Acknowledgements

I would like to thank the following people, whose help and contribution I have very much appreciated:

Richard

Stephen

Ros

Louise

Contents

Prologue

Words

Before the hammer blow fell on that fateful Saturday, Seef was with Staszek on the Friday evening. He was the Polish builder who flew over a few times a year to work for Seef. Staszek was leaving to fly back later that night. They sat down together in the lounge.

"How did you get on with the roof today?" asked Seef.

"I think I fix it okay. Is no okay for long time but is okay for short long time. It will be now I think well."

"Can water still get in through the roof?" asked Seef.

Staszek looked puzzled. "I no understand."

"Will rain come in the house?" tried Seef again.

"I think she will no come. She go to plastic and cement and will cross."

Seef didn't understand what he meant. "Plastic and cement and will cross?"

There was a pause. "I can't explain. I think is no well - but now it will be well," he said with a smile. Now Seef looked even more puzzled.

"Don't think about roof." said Staszek. "She must no come. Everything will be okay. Don't think. I shell you next time."

Seef knew that by 'shell', Staszek meant 'show'. But although communications were tricky, Seef always felt that Staszek had the 'Polish ingenuity' to get over problems in ways English workmen had forgotten about years ago.

"We go to the sing now?" asked Staszek.

They got out the folk guitars and sang a mixture of Polish, Slovak, Czech, Irish, gospel and western songs. They kept their voices oiled with beer and a little Polish vodka with generous amounts of coke. Then they stopped for a rest.

"Cards?" asked Seef.

They started to play a kind of Pontoon, with little bets of loose change. Several rounds were played. Seef thought he had enough low number cards for the 'five card trick', and threw in all his remaining change. Staszek thought the same for his hand. He held a five, a two and a four. All was resting on the next card, and it would have to be the last hand – it was getting near the time for Staszek to go. He put some more coins down – a picture card would give him the required twenty one.

They both watched for what the 'buy' would be. Staszek reached over – and drew the Jack of Hearts! He stood up and using the card to scoop the money, pocketed the whole lot.

"It will be just correct for train ticket!" he laughed as he went and gathered up his case and things. "I no need about next place. Gosia - he meet me in Poland." Gosia was his daughter, but he always mixed genders up. She was probably meeting him at the airport.

Language and words were an odd thing, thought Seef. He had had some crazy mix-ups with Staszek.

What about 'God's Word', the Bible? He never had it that clear in his head in what sense it could be. He knew that Staszek and he had frequent misunderstandings on jobs. They didn't always comprehend each other very well. If God was going to have a communication system, it would have to be better than that. All the different Bible versions! Did it matter? Was the message the same? He scratched his head. "Lord, help me understand words better. Help me understand *your* word. I don't want to *mis*understand, like I do with Staszek," he breathed.

Seef drove him to the train station. They said goodbye for the next couple of months. Then Seef went home to bed. That night he prayed for Staszek and for himself, for whatever would befall in his life; that it would be 'well'.

The next morning Seef was writing some notes for a little talk he was giving the following week – 'The Word' – it was for a fellowship group he met with. Earlier still he'd been playing Patience, a game he hardly bothered about, but he had come across the pack of cards again and was testing himself to see if he could remember the rules. (However he had the frustration of finding out that a card was missing.) It's funny how, later, he could remember all the details of what he had been doing that day; the last 'normal' day for a while; the lunch, the sketch of a spandrel he fancied carving, and so on. All to be laid aside and eclipsed by what was coming. All to be overshadowed because there was a deeper shadow approaching. All the normal things frozen like that when the doorbell rang. The talk would never be given, and the patience never finished, and the spandrel design would have to wait.

It's a rotten job sometimes being in the police. A policeman's lot is not, indeed, a happy one. Certainly for the two outside Seef Able's door that day. As the bell rang, it had just occurred to Seef, when he was on his way to answer the door, that it was Staszek who must have put the Jack of Hearts in his pocket with the money.

"The thieving, thoughtless scamp! Call the cops!" he found himself saying out loud just as he opened the front door.

"Mr. Seth Able, son of Mr. Sebastian Able of Amen House at Kings Sternton?"

"Sorry, yes. I was thinking of something else just then."

"May we come in, sir?"

"Of course."

They stood in the lounge. Playing cards, the washing up, the drawings for the spandrel, and notes for the 'Word' talk were all over the table.

"How can I help you?" said Seef.

They introduced themselves. Then they said, "I'm afraid we have some bad news concerning your father Mr. Sebastian Able. When did you last see him?"

"About two weeks ago. What's happened?"

"Sadly, I have to tell you that he has been found dead."

"Dead? Oh no!" Seef groaned. He stared at the policeman. "Was it his heart?"

13

"No, I'm very sorry to say he appears to have been murdered."

Was this real? What was he hearing? He fell back onto a chair.

"What? Murdered! Good Lord! Are you serious?"

"I'm afraid so. May we sit down and ask you a few questions?"

Seef waved them to chairs, and after a moment began answering their questions in a daze. His mind was in turmoil. Murdered! His own father! How could this be?

A notebook was produced and they began to explain. They had heard from someone who lived next door. "A Mr. Nayaboor, a Chinese gentleman..."

"That's Mi," interrupted Seef.

"...who apparently knew the deceased, had called round to see him, but there was no reply. He had previously noticed your father's sheep was lying in the garden, not moving. So he had kept his dog on its lead when he called and as he stood waiting at the front door, his dog kept barking at the door in a mysterious manner. He decided to call the police. When we broke in, sir," explained the officer, "we found your father in a pool of blood on the hall floor."

14

"Oh no, my poor dad," cried Seef.

"We're so sorry," said the police officer. "Is there anything we can do for you? Can we make you a cup of tea?"

"What? Oh no. I don't know what to do. Can I go to the house?"

"I'm afraid it's still a crime scene, sir. It will be available in two weeks. I should add that we found the sheep was also dead."

"That was 'Weelike', his pet sheep. What about the lamb?"

"The lamb is still alive. And you can go to the garden if you want – not the house. The Chinese gentleman is keeping an eye on the small lamb, which is grazing in the garden. But I'm afraid the house itself is off limits until we have completed our investigations. That will be about fourteen days, as I said, sir. Then you can have access. I'm so sorry, sir."

"In that case I will stay here and go in two weeks to Kings Sternton and Amen House, and see Mr. Nayaboor," said Seef. "It is kind of him to help. I did meet him a few times. Yes, he was a good friend of my father's. But oh, my poor father. Murdered! I can't believe it!"

There was a pause.

"Are you sure about that cup of tea?"

"Yes - no thanks - I just need time to let this shock sink in."

"Of course. Well, once again, we're sorry to be the bearers of this tragic news. We will keep in touch as to any progress we make in our investigations," the officer added as they both got up and began to move towards the door.

After the front door closed behind them, Seef fell against the hall wall. He made as if to strike the wall hopelessly with his fist. Then he began to sob. "Oh dad," he cried, "how can this have happened to a gentle soul like you? Who could have done such a thing?"

He paced around the house in an aimless manner. He began thinking about his father and him bravely managing without his mum, who had died the previous year, and then recalling his own last visit, and some of the random things they had talked about.

His dad had spoken about some of the practical problems in the house; such as various leaks and bits of rot, and Seef said he would arrange to get some things done for him. 'Weelike' the sheep and her lamb had kept the grass down in the garden, and when that was low he had put her and the lamb in the field, though access had sometimes been awkward with the neighbour.

His father said he had only recently begun using the field he owned once again, which was at the bottom of the garden, and which lay beyond the back fence. He hadn't got direct access, but he had a right of way by a path across the corner of his neighbour's garden. Seef had suggested that it might be better to let 'Weelike' and the lamb go and to concentrate on looking after himself and maybe the problems in the house.

"Oh no," said his father, "your mother loved Weelike. I couldn't do that."

After that they had had more talk about the heating deficiencies and the plumbing idiosyncrasies, but after a while his father had got bored, and instead started reminiscing about the old days and how he and Seef's mother had met at the Methodist mission, and then what the mission was like and what was said, and about what they did, and other things of that sort. He said there were a lot of differences between church life then and now.

Mostly Seef had heard it before, but he sat and smiled at his dad while he talked. He respected his father and realised that day he loved him dearly with all his eccentricities. He had been a wonderful dad. Then later they said what was to be their last goodbye. And now – horror of horrors – he was dead – actually murdered! Never to tell of those old days again.

Chapter One

Seef's background was architecture and building. He had worked for a long time in various architectural practices, beginning with tracing and then drawing plans for the upgrading of old railway stations and station hotels around the country. Later, he worked on layouts of various modern housing estates and new building designs of many different kinds. He had also worked on some radical architecture for a new town, and later restoring and changing some old Crown Court buildings and prison cells. He had actually covered a vast range of different architectural projects.

Then later, he had turned more to building management and for a while been in charge of different building sites. For quite a long time he had run his own company and even 'took to the tools', when there wasn't much other work. He had always been reasonable at carpentry and that phase of his working life culminated in him building a complete house of a wood construction. Just before that he had been working on hotel and conference facilities with new kitchens. That was a challenge, because the hotel was in constant use.

When Seef looked back, he was rather surprised to reflect on what he had fitted into his career overall and the unusual variety of all the experiences he had come through in the industry. And somehow he always felt that one half of him was a (hopefully!) discerning architect while the other was an ordinary practical builder.

Now, with the latest tragic news and both his parents gone, he realised that he was left with all his parents' possessions and money (being without siblings) and their large old dilapidated house and grounds. He had to decide what to do with it all. After the shock of the murder, he prayed about all these things (he always tried to remember to do that) and then he re-thought his next few years through. A lot of changes would have to be made. He began to make many preparations.

He knew that at some point he had the flight booked with the airline to Bewlar. The arrangement was a kind of an open ticket, dependent on when there was space. They would call for him when they were ready and he would then go to the airport straight away. But it could be a long, long time before he got that call. It was possible it might be next week, but it was much more likely to be quite a few years. It was an odd arrangement, but he had known about it for a long time. Bewlar sounded like a wonderful place for a real retirement and in some ways he looked forward to it. But for most of the time he simply forgot about it, like a pension plan you put away in a drawer and never bother to look at.

Seef had decided, after several days' thought and prayer, that he would go to live in Kings Sternton for a few years, perhaps longer. He had a few good friends where he was living, but thought he would come back from time to time and stay a week in his old home. He could close the house up in between times. There would still be council tax to pay but the property itself was appreciating in value. He didn't want the bother of letting it. He'd done that years before and it would be a lot of hassle and work. He decided it would be a better use of his time to invest his money as well as he could in the markets and meantime potter about with odd jobs at Amen House, up in Kings Sternton.

He would also do a bit more on his studies and writing and arrange for some of the larger building jobs at his father's old place to be done. He would contact Staszek about that. There was a small church in the village and he would be able to make a few new friends and renew acquaintances. It would be nice to see the lamb grazing out the back. He then thought about the materials, tools and plant he would need.

So it was that Seef made up his mind that he would 'semi-retire' and that he would work at his own pace with Staszek on the old house. He always liked Amen House and felt it had great potential. It was a large project, all considered, but then he liked a challenge and felt it would be a chance to put some of his imagined ideas for the place into practice. In fact he had just the right experience to do such a thing, because he was both an architectural designer and a practical kind of jack-of-all-trades builder and his health generally was pretty tolerable.

Thus, after he was allowed access by the police, he moved into the old place. He would be able to keep up-to-date more easily with the police enquiries. He was still feeling eaten up inside by the thought of who could have done it.

Once at the house he began to look at the jobs about him. However, within a few days he seriously re-considered his proposal. There was much more work to do than he had ever anticipated. He had hoped to launch straight into a new porch and canopy right across the front, which he had always fancied would set off the whole architectural appearance of the front elevation. To him, it had always 'cried out' for the roofs at the two sides to be linked together in such an arrangement. During the first drive up to the old house he had almost planned the whole thing out in his head and even the materials required, and so he stepped out of the car actually holding a measuring tape in his hand ready to get an idea of the roof spans required and the length of the timbers.

But as he shut the door of the car that first day, his hopes were dashed immediately – as he glanced up at the roofscape of the front elevation – for he immediately noticed a problem with the integrity of the old roof that was staring at him right in the face. Certainly a leak there. He realised that *that* would have to be put right first, and went in to the hall ready to go upstairs and begin to inspect the situation, but as he walked through the passage he noticed the floor boards in the hall also needed immediate attention. This hadn't really been noticed before, but the police had arranged for the old carpet to be stripped out – it was badly stained, they said – and the sight of the decrepit boards beneath, which were about to collapse, now greeted him in the hall. In one place a board had actually broken and was now sticking up. It didn't look as if the police had been very careful. The other boards were half rotten with a previous wet-rot. This was quite shocking. It was a wonder his parents hadn't actually fallen through years ago!

Now you mustn't imagine Seef was ready to despair at this point. You should remember that he had been dealing with these kinds of problems all his life and he knew exactly what was required practically. It's just that he knew these things would take a lot longer than he originally thought, and he felt a little miffed that he wouldn't be able to start the porch and canopy that he wanted, for quite a while.

Meantime, while he was looking about and still had his coat on, and as it wasn't raining, Seef decided to look at the garden. He noticed the sheep and her lamb had kept the grass down – more or less – and also had shortened what was left of the flowerbeds! He walked down the garden to look at the field. He could see over into the pretty grassed area where the lamb was apparently grazing contentedly. Seef was glad that it had appeared to get over losing its mother.

The access to the field across the corner of the

neighbour's garden didn't look as if it were 'open'. A wide plough had been drawn right across the path as if to deter access. He wondered whether to climb over the plough and go to the field, but thought he'd leave it for now. Seef looked at the lamb. Now it was looking up and taking note of Seef, but shortly resumed its grazing. Seef looked at the plough. It looked as if someone had been working on it and a part might be needed, since it didn't look complete. Probably it had broken and they hadn't been able to pull it out of the way.

He went back to the house and looked again at the problem of the hall flooring. It was certainly rotten. As a temporary measure he would get some ply or something out of the shed later so that at least people could walk through safely. He looked under the broken board that was sticking up. There appeared to be a large void underneath, and he couldn't even see down into it properly. Surely there was a concrete sub-floor in place? Probably not, though. He remembered another old house he had worked on, where, in the dining room, there was nothing – just a space – then the ground itself! Well, it was another thing to be investigated later. He would certainly book Staszek to come up for as long as possible on his next visit to England.

Chapter Two

Food

Later that day Seef went and tapped on Mi's door. After a minute Mi appeared at the door surrounded by steam and smoke.

"Ha! I cooking, Mr. Seef, I cooking! Come in."

Seef followed him back into his kitchen.

"What are you cooking?"

"I cook fried rice, Chinese style!"

"Oh! Sounds nice."

"You have some of my rice. You sit there. I give you." He paused. "Mr Seef, I so sorry about your father."

"Thank you. I was calling to say I appreciated your help in looking after the lamb and everything you've done for me in this sad case."

"Oh, it was nothing. Sit down, I tell you about it. Then you eat my special fried rice."

"I would like to hear, but I can't trouble you about food."

"You just drive here?"

"Yes, more or less."

"Then you need food. But I tell you what I know. There is not much to tell really."

Mi then told how he and Seef's father met up once or twice a week. It was on returning from one of Mi's walks alone with his dog that he noticed 'Weelike', Seef's father's sheep, lying still in the garden and the lamb standing bleating next to her. There was no sign of his friend, so he decided to knock on the door. There was no reply, but his dog kept barking at the door in a strange way – so he decided to call the police. Then they came and broke in, and he heard the terrible news from them of how they found his friend, dead. Mi looked again at the son before him, who reminded him very much of his old friend.

"I so sorry, Mr. Seef."

"I still can't believe it," said Seef.

"You must look to Lord for strength," said Mi. "He will sustain you. Get through and look to Him. Meantime keep strength up and come and eat."

It was actually just the right thing for Seef at that moment. He didn't want to listen to more sympathy – he'd already had that from acquaintances at home – but he *was* hungry just at that moment. He'd hardly eaten anything but snacks and bits since the police had called that day with the news.

"How do you cook your fried rice?" asked Seef.

"First I use 'seasoned' wok – this one here – I put butter or oil in and put on heat, then fry eggs, whipping them up quick. I chop this egg up with my shovel and serve onto plate at side. Next I rinse wok and begin again with high heat. Add oil. I fried some chopped red onion and garlic and ginger today, but I sometimes use white onion if I have. I added chopped chilli – green and red – because I like it hot – hope you do."

"Oh yes!" said Seef.

"Then I add chopped vegetables, today it was coloured peppers, broccoli and carrot strips. This is what I cooking when you come, so now I finish. Your father, he loved my fried rice." Mi turned the gas to high. "Next I add salt and pepper and Chinese five spice. Here is my rice, cold from fridge. This go in next."

He put the rice in and began flattening it and turning it about with his 'shovel'. He then got his willow pattern plates out. "This my favourite plates," he said. "I always wanted garden like this with little bridges and boats! Now more to add to rice! Today I use chopped ham and chicken pieces; this I got ready before. And also today I add drained tuna and Thai fish sauce for saltiness. Not always I do this, but I like flavour. In China and Thailand, fish sauce is used for sour with all meats. So I put pinch of sugar now for sweet! A few chopped small tomatoes go in and frozen peas. Last I add back egg, and soy sauce, and these chopped green spring onions."

He worked the steaming mass around while the delicious smell wafted around the kitchen toward Seef.

"Now I ready to serve!" cried Mi. "Here it come!" He piled some in the two bowls.

"Thank you Lord for this," said Mi. "Please help Seef with everything. Amen."

Spoons were produced and they began to tuck in. The formula worked. Mi had been right. After two bowls of this – Mi gave him more – Seef felt a lot better. Afterwards Seef pushed his chair back from the table. He felt much better and much more relaxed.

"So you've been at the Parish Church in the village for a long time now?" he said to Mi.

"Yes. But I leaving now, Mr. Seef."

"Oh! What's happening?"

"I go to St Joseph's and the Holy Child in Duxton."

"The Roman Catholic church?"

"Yes. I told lady vicar here. I like R.C. and high; bell and smell I think it is called!"

"Oh yes, St Joe's. I've been there once or twice."

"They believe in miracles, Mr. Seef. This important. I think, 'King of our Hearts' must be Lord of all our life, so we believe Him for natural *and* supernatural. Better to have faith same as apostles. Everything up in air for Anglicans I find. They want to be modern and materialistic and too much like world."

"Yes, probably a lot of them."

Seef could identify. He'd been concerned about the liberalisation of the Church of England for a while himself.

"Well you could well be onto something Mi. The liberals have got their big feet in the door, questioning Scripture, embracing the world's science and values; like all this business of equality with gays and transgenders! And even the archbishop is saying it's fine for boys to be wearing ballet dresses and high heels! The church *is* getting like the world. (I saw recently that the boys who are in the girl guides – that's a joke! – should be allowed to shower with the girls if they *feel* like they are girls!) The founders of the C of E will be turning in their graves!"

"I agree. They should get back, Mr. Seef, to Bible, and to historic, apostolic, supernatural, Christian faith.

But church must be careful, because there are a very few children (and adults) who are really confused about their gender. I know someone like this, Mr. Seef. Also I know exceptions *mustn't* make the rules. The world (and modernisers in the church), are making it worse, because they look like they are tolerant of gender mixing.

"Bible says people must not 'cross-dress'. It's a sin! And it may be a temptation to be 'opposite', you know? However, ones who are confused, but repentant, need help to find forgiveness and be their true gender – the one God gave them at birth. If they have 'Y' chromosome, they are boy! Having operations to change gender, doesn't fix anything, only healing through Jesus Christ. Following the Bible and prayer is what this twisted world needs. Jesus will heal, Mr. Seef!"

"Amen! You see Mi, I think it should be a combination of – oh, I don't know how to explain it well – but it's to be the entire Bible and all what you just said: apostolic and supernatural. The Bible should be our primary revelation. But then these modernising wallies get hold of Scripture and change it about – they subtly change the text and omit bits – so we need apostolic teaching, tradition and the Holy Spirit too. You know they twist the Scripture and 'reduce' it and 'contextualise' it until it's unrecognisable. So we have to keep both the Catholic and Pentecostal side.

"I like what Richard Hooker, the founder of the Anglican Church said. He said what was number 1 – what Scripture *plainly* 'delivers', then number 2 – what can be *reasoned* from Scripture, and lastly, number 3 – what Hooker called the 'voice of the church', by which he meant what the church has said in all places and times. So there you would get the early church and apostolic writings; the books of Jasher and Enoch, then the early fathers and doctors, the medieval church, the Reformed, the Catholic and modern Protestant as all part of that 'choir' as it were – and Hooker said it was a voice to be listened to very lovingly. So in today's language that would mean the liberal theologians (who spent more of their time reading the Guardian and listening to the BBC and Channel 4!) would listen to the apostles and early saints etc. – and the African churches! That would help 'em!"

Seef put his finger to his lips. "I'd better not say any more – I feel my hobby horses are galloping out apace," he said. "My wild tongue! Let's change the subject! How did you get to know my dad, Mi?"

"He was friendly when I first came here. He help me even with my name, you know?"

"Your name?"

"Yes, when I first came to England I was wondering what name I could have because my Chinese name unpronounceable in English. I suggest to your father 'Mankind' because I am Man and I am Kind! He said that was quite good, but then he asked me to say my name in Chinese. When I did he said it sounded a bit like 'neighbour', which is a word English people would know. And he said it go well with Mi, like 'my neighbour'."

"Ha ha, very good. I like it." Seef paused. He remembered hearing that Mi had a small problem with his roof. "Do you want to show me about your roof? Maybe you can show me in case it could leak."

"Oh yes, but no hurry to do anything remember. You are busy."

Mi led him through to a room at the back. When he saw it, he could hardly believe how Mi could have put up with it. There was an inch or two of water all over the floor, the plasterboard was hanging down from the ceiling and above that were some roof tiles which were clearly not doing their job. He could even see patches of sky through the gaps.

"Oh dear Mi. This looks bad. I think I'll try and pop round later and sheet it over."

"Thank you so much, Mr. Seef. You are kind."

"Thank *you* for helping out my dad over the years. I know you did."

"It was no problem. By way, woman called Jez, your father's other next door neighbour, buried his dead pet sheep, 'Weelike', after police looked and finished."

"Jez? Oh, I'll have to see her, too. Well anyway, thank you. I think I'll call the lamb, 'Weelike the Second'. This was another name my father invented – it was from Handel's Messiah: 'We like sheep have gone astray.'"

"Oh! I didn't know this. Very true of humanity!" exclaimed Mi.

Seef then decided to head back to find some sheeting for Mi's repair and at least keep further water out.

Chapter Three

The Word

Seef was a Christian, but he didn't consider himself a 'churchman'. He was committed to Christ, but not especially to any church. He always considered that church just happened to be the place Christians met. Once he had described himself as an 'Evangelical in his head', (why head? – well that intellectual part of his faith was kind of easy to explain), a 'Catholic in his legs', (why legs? – well sometimes his legs led him to take mass there, or any miracle-believing church!) and a 'Pentecostal in his heart', (why heart? – well he had got converted in Pentecostalism). When he was at Kings Sternton he had the same habit – he went where he felt led. So it was, that a few days after seeing Mi, Seef went along to the local parish church for the Sunday service.

His house, his neighbours and his church were situated in what used to be called a 'hamlet' of about a dozen or so houses, which had a very small Anglican church. Kings Sternton church, he learned, had been built about two hundred years earlier by a local benefactor who had started what became a famous national company, which was later taken over by an international conglomerate. They were now nothing to do with Kings Sternton, though one or two of the family still lived there and supported the church a bit financially he had heard.

The congregation that morning was small of course and most of them quite elderly. Genesis chapter four was the reading and they read the whole chapter. Seef was quite surprised they read the whole chapter out, especially as it was the King James Version, because the last part seemed to begin a series of 'begats', which were the parts he normally skipped over when he read Genesis himself. The sermon, however, was based only on verses 6 and 7:

"Why art thou wroth? And why is thy countenance fallen? If thou doest not well, sin lieth at the door."

The lady who was vicar tried to bring it to apply to situations people can face today. She said we can get angry and adopt a negative demeanour – which shows up in our face! It was better to do our best with God's help, even if we felt like tearing our hair out. It would be 'well' if we did that, and we would have peace. But if we got 'stressed' then we're very likely to have the perception that we're not doing well – and sin then lies 'at our door'. Someone could say the smallest thing to upset us – and it would push us over the edge – and we lash out. Just that week, she said, she had met someone who was 'stressed out' – over nothing really. It was an event that was coming up, and *they* wanted everything to be right, but it wasn't quite to *their* satisfaction somehow, and so they – this person – began – of all things – to really criticise other people and actually judge them for their inadequacies. So, concluded the vicar in her sermon, we can get to sin because we think it isn't 'well', and yet it can begin over nothing much in reality.

Seef began to think back and saw that this could apply to one or two of his own situations. If he allowed anger in – it became easy to sin. He *was* feeling angry himself that his father's murderer was still on the loose, and thus far the police seemed to have got nowhere.

Seef talked with the vicar afterwards and thanked her and after she extended her sympathy she explained about the 'sharing of services' system around there. She was in charge of another parish too and had been given seven small country churches to look after as well. So she spent most of the week, and especially Sundays, tearing from place to place. There was a rota so that not all of them had a service – or sometimes one was taken by a reader or volunteer. She inquired after Seef's arrangements and found out a bit about him – before launching back onto her favourite hobby horse.

"It is a ridiculous job," she said. "My husband, who was doing this job before me, had a nervous breakdown doing it, and now I'm having to nurse him as well. What with the baptisms, marriages and funerals and the various PCC and diocese meetings, it's crazy – there are umpteen pastoral responsibilities too. And the building maintenance! All the church buildings are old and most feature halls and old meeting rooms and ancient facilities etc. I sometimes think I'll go mad. And we're haemorrhaging our congregations! As I say, it's ridiculous just keeping up with it all, never mind doing anything worthwhile."

"Oh, that's a pity," said Seef. He could see that she might have her own temptations to be cross about what she'd been saddled with.

"I don't suppose you fancy a bit of travelling churchwarden duty?" she asked hopefully.

"It's very difficult at the moment," said Seef.

They must have been quite desperate, because later a man approached him who turned out to be Frank, the 'acting' churchwarden. It wasn't long before he too asked Seef if he might have any spare time for building jobs now that he was living in the village.

"I'm afraid I'm only just finding my feet and I've discovered I've got a major task to keep a roof over my head," Seef replied. He noticed that lay, non-building people, didn't distinguish much between architects and builders. Seef *was* actually rather unusual in his experience and practice.

"Oh well, never mind," the warden said. "Just thought I'd ask, just in case. I'm finding everything a stretch. Have you met the amazing Josh?"

A young man of striking appearance stood near to them whom Seef had noticed during the service. After he had introduced them the warden moved off.

"Got to go and see someone at St Mark's!" Frank said in parting.

Josh turned out to be a Jewish convert to Christianity who lived in the hamlet. Seef had been talking to him for a while and finding out that what he was saying was rather fascinating somehow - when some other people came over to barge in, and walked up to Seef to introduce themselves. Josh slipped away.

"Are you our new builder neighbour?" said the first

lady. "I'm Jez Cane."

Jez was a fairly well built woman of about forty. She was crop headed with a rather ugly scar across her forehead. With her was her husband and a younger girl of about eighteen. Also there was Mi.

"Hello Mrs Cane," said Seef. "Yes, I'm your neighbour, and I worked in both architecture and building."

"Ah good. But please, call me Jez. Only we've got a couple of jobs need doing! This is my incompetent husband, George, and our lovely lodger, Lily."

Lily was an attractive, younger blonde with red lipstick. Jez then began to explain in some detail how a pane of glass in her conservatory at the back of her house had developed a crack and needed immediately replacing and that also the tap was leaking. She added that her husband was useless at that sort of thing.

"You've met Frank, our neurotic warden, I think. He has damp underparts I believe, but he's had them for ages!"

"Well I might be able to have a quick call round for you but I don't always get involved in those sort of things."

"We can't get anyone to come out here," she said.

"It's so difficult to get repairs done. I could send my silly husband to you if we need bits, but *do* come round yourself soon, if you would. We'll probably see you next week then?"

"Well, as I say, I'll see what I can do."

"I always say *I* can achieve anything I set my mind to, always provided I can explain it and train my hopeless husband!" she laughed. George just stood there, smiling meekly.

Seef then turned and told Mi, who was nearby, that he'd call and see him again. Next he looked around to see if Josh was still about but he was talking to someone else. Seef managed to catch his eye.

"Come round sometime," he mouthed. Josh smiled back. Seef was thinking that he'd like to chat again with him. He was curious about some of the things he'd said. He then made his way over to the side where he'd spied a steaming teapot and some slices of cake. An elderly lady introduced herself.

"I'm Mrs Welch."

"I'm Seef Able."

"Pleased to meet yer," she said. "'Ow d'yer 'ave yer tea, luv?"

"Quite strong please."

"There yer go. Do 'ave some carrot cake ducks. I made it fresh yesterday. There's plenty, look."

Just then there was a stir at the back of the church. Two gentlemen and a lady were making their way in.

"Big bad Jim and Monkey Boy," said Mrs Welch. "That there Jim's 'oo we're be'olden to, 'e is. Pays the 'lectric on this place. He don't come often."

Big Jim and Boy made their way in, nodding at acquaintances. The vicar immediately broke away from someone else and began talking to them. Jim was perfectly manicured; his grey hair perfectly styled. Monkey Boy, a nicely built lad of forty-five or so, with a shaven bullet head, stood alongside Jim, like a bodyguard. And on the other side was an older woman whom Seef hadn't really noticed at first. She was heavily made up and looked like she'd been through the mill, yet she had some authority in her countenance somehow. She stood slightly behind and was whispering to Jim. It was Monkey Boy's mother. Her name, Seef learned later, was Rosemary. Jim himself was leaning on his expensive-looking cane. He had several large rings and a jewel on his tie pin. He was looking curiously and nervously towards Josh.

Seef found himself staring at Big Jim's walking-

42

stick. It was heavy, with silver and brass parts. Seef realised that it could be a terrible weapon in the hands of someone who wanted to hurt you. It was probably something just like that walking-stick that had killed his father. All it would take is a moment of anger, when sin happened to lay at the door.

Seef glanced at Big Jim's face. He had a rather ugly, fixed-face smile while he seemed to be listening to the vicar, but his watchful eyes were darting this way and that, especially towards Josh. Suppressed anger was there, thought Seef. There was something cruel in those eyes. Seef wondered what his dead father had thought of him, or if he'd known him. Perhaps if they had been slight acquaintances he might have invited him in – and then his dad might have said the wrong thing...

"Does Big Jim live round here?" asked Seef of Mrs Welch.

"King's Lodge. The big 'ouse," said Mrs Welch. "We ought to say it's an honour to 'ave 'im supportin' us really. But... Any 'ows, Big Bad Jim don't come 'ere much. 'E never comes to service, but 'e likes to see what's 'appening. 'E's the grandson of the big business people who lived 'ere years ago. Got a few bob! I think 'e likes people to know 'e's the benefactor, like. Monkey

Boy is 'is son. That's 'is name from when he used to tear round the village years ago! The Boy's devoted to 'is dad, 'e is. But (I shouldn't be a tellin' ya really), 'e's got a bit of a record with the law. I think violence runs in the family."

"How long have you been here Mrs Welch?"

"Forty years, but I've already told the vicar I'm switching to join me friend at the Pentecostal in Duxton."

"Are you?"

"Yes, they do all the good ole 'ims, and 'ave gospel like I'm used to from years ago. It's a bit dead 'ere I reckons. And I don't go for all this 'ere political correctness or whatever they calls it. Though I likes the vicar lady."

"Oh yes, I think I understand where you are coming from," said Seef.

"Well we 'ad just the straight 'word' and repentance, and thanks and worship o' Jesus years ago! But not so much now wiv them there C of E bishops in their nighties going on about queer sex - so I told the vicar straight, I did. Anyway 'ave some cake luv."

"I'm not mad on cake thanks – but now a bacon sandwich – that would be something else!"

"I'll remember that ducks, that I will," she said with a wink. "I'll do ya one next week – if yer 'ere!"

"Who is the lady with Mr. Jim?" asked Seef.

"That's Rosemary, that is. Monkey Boy's mother. They never married, 'er and Big Bad Jim. She 'ad dosh, but 'ad an 'ard life with 'im I always say. Some say she always wears 'eavy makeup to cover up where 'e's 'it 'er! 'E's got a nasty temper when sommat's upset 'im. But anyhows it's none of me business, so I best not say more. What I do know is she tried to pack up drinking and to come to their Bible study 'ere once, but Big Jim soon stopped her doing anythink like that. So I say she's 'ad an 'ard life with a man like 'im. Sorry luv. I shouldn't 'ave said all that to ya, but I feels for 'er even if she's not short o' money."

Seef nodded to Mrs Welch. "I won't say anything," he whispered. Then he finished his tea and made his way out of the church with a wave. As he walked away he was trying to remember some lyrics from an old Dylan song that had suddenly come into his head when he heard the name 'Big Jim'. That's right; it was '*Lily, Rosemary and the Jack of Hearts*.' How did it go now?

Big Jim was no one's fool, he owned the town's only diamond mine.

He made his usual entrance, looking so dandy
and so fine,
With his bodyguard and his silver cane and
every hair in place.
He took whatever he wanted to and he laid it all
to waste -
But his bodyguard and his silver cane were no
match for the Jack of Hearts.

That was it! And a perfect match too! But who would be the Jack of Hearts in this context? No doubt about that! The Jack of Hearts would be Josh. There was something altogether superior about him all right. Seef tried to remember another verse from the song. About a 'Lily' he thought it was. Yes, Lily was the blonde with red lipstick that he'd just seen. He remembered,

She'd come away from a broken home had lots
of strange affairs
With men in every walk of life which took her
everywhere.
But she'd never met anyone quite like the Jack
of Hearts.

It fitted! Even the names! How strange!

Yes that's even how Seef himself felt about Josh, even from their quick meeting that morning. Seef had been to lots of places and met many people (and had a good imagination!) but somehow he felt quite sure he'd never met anyone quite like the Jack of Hearts himself! Even from his brief encounter there was something in Josh's look, something in his demeanour that made you want to listen. It was a quiet authority, that's what it was. And yet he was humble too – but he was probably a nobody. Odd, that. As he walked home, Seef heard a birdsong. He felt a whistle coming on, so he didn't hold back. He looked a cheerful sight as he made his way home to lunch. Then he suddenly remembered another verse from the song.

> Rosemary combed her hair and took a carriage into town.
> She slipped into the side door looking like a queen without a crown.
> She fluttered her false eyelashes and whispered in his ear,
> "Sorry darlin' that I'm late," but he didn't seem to hear.
> He was staring into space over at the Jack of Hearts
>
> "I know I've seen that face before," Big Jim was thinking to himself;
> Maybe down in Mexico, or a picture upon somebody's shelf...

Now, *that* is uncanny, thought Seef. A Rosemary too! He walked on, imagining if the details of the lives he'd just seen lined up further with the song. As he walked he realised that actually the song didn't quite line up with the characters completely. But did Jim kill someone? He couldn't remember. No - the names of others weren't quite the same anyway. Of course it didn't line up and they weren't the same! The Jack of Hearts was a bank robber in the song! Like a thief in the night! Well, Jesus would only take what was His! In the song, the Jack of Hearts had accomplices, who, while he was in the bar with Big Jim and Lily and Rosemary, were 'drilling in the wall', perhaps from Lily's dressing room, in order to rob the bank! Then there was a character in it who was a 'hanging judge' – and so on. The song wasn't prophetic about Kings Sternton! How could it be?

No, it just happened to be a good little story that had been written up by a poet with some talent. But it was a much different case with the Bible, surely? Yes indeed, that was written – Seef couldn't imagine how – by the Spirit of God who took certain men and lifted them up into his service in some way to write. Now that *was* supernatural, prophetic and actually inerrant. It was maybe a little bit like that with the apocryphal books, like Enoch and the Book of Jasher. They were not canon of course. However, not to say that it's only the Bible that has prophetic manifestations and utterances. Certainly not! Anyone could be inspired to be used by God. But the Scriptures themselves *were* unique. Miraculous, actually. But how and where?

The miraculous! He remembered hearing how, in the Azusa Street Revival, the Spirit had used men and women to say things in the services which were the *exact* details of people's personal lives, only known to them alone, and when they had heard these words, they were so convicted that they had gone down on their knees and got instantly converted. And it had often led to supernatural healings. Why, people had actually grown whole arms and legs! So it was possible that real prophecy and miracles occurred outside the Bible. God used whom He wanted. He used kings and rulers for His purposes if He wanted to, like say, Cyrus.

God used nature too. Why shouldn't He? It was His! He designed it. He invented the maths and the physics that lay behind the universe and dreamed up what kept the whole show on the road. If it hadn't been designed to those exact specifications it would have simply collapsed. Numbers were His too. He invented numbers! So for example, when certain number sequences were plotted onto a graph, you could get something like the

49

'Mandelbrot Set'. The Mandelbrot Set! It had only been discovered about 1980, Seef thought. Numbers were amazing. He had a friend who loved prime numbers and went around working out sequences of them in his head.

He remembered that the Mandelbrot Set were pairs of numbers you plotted out on a graph – he wasn't sure how it worked exactly – maybe like the Fibonacci Sequence of numbers – but, it had been discovered that when you plotted the Mandelbrot Set on a graph on a computer, you got a pattern which made a kind of fractal. A fractal that could be infinitely shrunk or magnified to produce the same repeating patterns. Incredible! Yes, God liked numbers and patterns! Well, why shouldn't He? He could like them if He wanted. It was all His own design, and He said of His creation, 'it was very good'.

Seef was getting closer to his house now. How many paces was it? He had no idea, but numbers could be fascinating. In the Mandelbrot Set you got this special shape, these patterns; like sometimes you got a spiral or a double spiral, sometimes a strange repeating sequence – like you had the 'valley of the sea horses' in it and the 'valley of the elephants' in it, which could be seen infinitely, if you had enough computing power. If?

Yes, and if you had enough computing power perhaps there would be patterns in the Bible too? Yes. There might very well be. Again – why not? Look at the DNA God designed! Why, life itself and the events in it make some kind of pattern don't they? A pattern that, at present, we only see from the back side, like the back of a cross-stitch. We see there all the threads and bits hanging out, some short or missing, some long. It was only when you turned it over you saw the design in it. In life also, if you got God's view, you could see the pattern of life's events. His dad's life had made such a pattern, but the thread had stopped. We might see the patterns when we get to heaven (that is, if we are God's friends and make it there).

As Seef was walking, he was passing the field where he could just about see Weelike the Second grazing. *We* were sheep and lambs, of course! Ignorant and stupid, stumbling around, unable to see the way ahead. What was the way ahead? Christ of course. But what was the way ahead for Seef now? To get this house done and see this murder solved and justice done. How to start then? Mmm. His stomach rumbled. Start with lunch of course! What? How about a glass of beer and an egg and bacon sandwich? He strode into his front garden. Yes, that would be a start anyway!

Over his beer and sandwich he sat looking out over the back garden. He could see Weelike the Second in the distance going at the grass contentedly but voraciously. That was how he wanted to be with the work on the property. He had to learn to be content with what he could achieve, yet work at it steadily and relentlessly to achieve his aim. It would help when Staszek got there.

Just then he thought he heard a strange sound coming from the hall. He walked out and stood there. Surely not? The hole in the floor! No. Crazy. He was mistaken. He went back and sat down.

But the murder of his father was something he couldn't let rest in his mind. He hoped, rather than expected, that the police were working tirelessly on the case. But they were probably doing nothing at all! It was frustrating. He would have to put it all out of his mind for now. He had found previously it was no good brooding on painful subjects. It was better if you could push it from your mind while you did something else that was interesting. Then, after you'd done that something else for a while, you might come back to that first thing – and you might feel less pain. What could that something else be for today that would hold his attention? The spandrels! These were the two decorative sort of triangular-shaped pieces that went above the arch that he planned to have over the entrance to the porch. He began to think out a really interesting design for them, a development of his previous ideas.

He wondered how God thought about creation when He designed and made it. All in six days! Did the numbers and physics make a pattern in His mind? However He did it, it was astonishing really. It was 'very good' – actually perfect. It was light years from something like his spandrel designs or a song story about Lily and Rosemary etc. by Dylan. And yet – God had endowed us with *some* creative talent – well, 'sub-creative' was what J R R Tolkien had called it, because God was the only true creator.

Also He could build on our stumblings and gropings. We might invent a pack of playing cards say – of course we could only do that with His help – but in God's mind every card had a meaning – perhaps not – or perhaps so, why not? And then of course it was easy for demonic beings (who had been given free will by Him just like us) to get hold of things and corrupt them. Like they did with our minds for example. Like they encouraged us to turn love into lust. Like they encouraged good desires to be perverted in some way. That's what we saw all over the place now, and it had even appeared in the church too...

Then again, like, say the twelve constellations in the night sky, which were originally designed to be good – and they actually told the gospel story – like them, things could be corrupted in men's minds and twisted, and pretty soon the legitimate message of the constellations had descended into the demonic arts of astrology, and, instead of people looking to God for guidance, they filled their heads with silly astrological nonsense and imagined that their foolish lives and loves were being controlled by the stars, or something like that.

So too, in a pack of cards or a tarot deck, people could see patterns and then they imagined all sorts of stupidity. And God let them! Why? Because He made them free, that's why. They ignored Him so they could sin, so He allowed them to fill their heads with nonsense and believe a lie. Just from cards! But not just cards actually – the people living in the world seemed to do such things with anything.

Cards were an example of how Seef had put a foot wrong once before in his past, gambling his few pence away at college, when he should have been studying.

Looking out for Kings and Aces and Jacks instead of reading. He should have turned to the real King for help, that way he would have been more like an Ace at things! And the Jack? Someone said that the Jack of Hearts was the equivalent of the Christ card; a sort of 'sacrifice card'. The lamb who was slain! Seef broke his chain of thought and looked out again at Weelike the Second in the field. He appeared at that moment to be staring straight at him. Rather unsettling.

That night Seef dreamed he was in a different house, but hearing the odd sound again. At one point he woke up and went and stood on the landing, above the hole in the hall floor. No - nothing. 'Get back to bed you silly man,' he told himself.

Chapter Four

Blood Sport

Another day altogether, a damp and cheerless morning. A day when the damp and cheerless air was doing its best to combine with the damp and cheerless ground. Wet and muddy everywhere. Along the road up the paths and into the very houses. The kind of wet and sticky mud that Peppa Pig and her young brother George (complete with his dinosaur) would have loved jumping around in! All damp and cheerless for us adults, but having the kind of wet and sticky mud that would have made Kings Sternton a welcome sight for half a dozen hippopotami and their little ones to come and have fun in. Indeed, it would not be a surprise to see them sporting in the low watery places alongside the road already. 'Mud, mud, glorious mud! There's nothing quite like it for cooling the blood.'

So who is this making his way along the village road towards the hamlet? Could it be a small hippo that had heard of the delights? No! It is only Dick Grub growling and moaning. His street cry of 'Can you 'elp me?' has evolved into 'C'yelp me?' He has deserted the refinements of his usual town residence and the hunting grounds in Duxton for a leisurely fact finding trip into the countryside this morning, and here he is! His sideways gait, and his ill fitting dirty and torn clothes and his bent back all coming along with him. He is unmistakeable even if we didn't hear his cry of approach from inside our houses.

And what has he been dining on today? There was an abandoned McDonalds on the ground for a starter. And he has been scavenging in the fields on his way up here. (The fish course had been omitted this morning due to a clean up by the chip shop.) A few raw carrots from the field were his second course and a gone-to-seed cabbage. Then for mains he had some luck today when he found a blackbird's nest. All the little greenish blue eggs – save the one he left for the mother bird – were gladly consumed, shells and all. Bon appétit, Monsieur Dick! 'But' he says to himself, 'there is a scarcity of nice titbits. I shall now go and explore my country retreat I believe.'

And so here he is, and he wonders what he can find in Kings Sternton today. Shall he enquire at the doors or not? Better not today, he thinks. He knows where there is a hen-house and some bird tables and hopes to borrow one or two eggs and a slice or two of bread. And so he works his way, as silently as he can, around the sheds and outbuildings at the bottom of the long gardens, disappearing where he can and exhibiting himself where he cannot.

The villagers know his habits and try to lock things or put them away, but most of them think it will be bad luck for them if they leave him nothing. They avoid him. They think he is a man who can easily turn to violence. But then they don't know him well enough, do they? They catch sight of him through their netted windows moving around, and imagine all sorts of things about him.

But what is this he has spied on his perambulation? A shed with some interesting items where he has been nicely supplied with wearables before. He fancies that certain accoutrements to add to his Sunday best may have been left there specifically for him, but in his line of work one can never be too sure. It is actually the shed at the bottom of Josh's garden. Josh is out today but this spot has certainly been a supplier of gentlemen's apparel in the past. Size is not usually a problem for Dick's thin frame. Ah! What is this? A decent waterproof coat with big pockets, some new wellingtons, and a nice selection of metal tools; a big garden knife, a metal dibber that will be useful for his gleaning of the fields of root crops. All useful stuff! He helps himself and fills his pockets. Then over to the old hen-coop. The hens don't seem to mind him, which is just as well, or their owners might have been alarmed. Dick Grub really seems to be at one with nature and the animals and he knows more about the outdoors than anyone around here. He loves the very trees and plants and all the animal life in his backyard. He thanks 'Abba Fadder' for each! He is a god-fearing country gent at heart is Mr Dick Grub.

He looks at another garden, where he has gleaned potatoes before now, which were roasted on a fire in the woods, but the tops of these potatoes all look black and dead. He finds a few old spuds among them, but they are not the best. He nevertheless tops up his pockets. A good job neighbour Jez is not looking! There is his friend the little lamb in the field. They greet each other; he gives it a carrot top.

"Where's your mudder sweetie," he says. "Where's Weelike then? And where's your shepherd master who gave me a shillin' or two?"

Back he goes along the village road. The children in the village shout out and tease him. He laughs. He makes as if to chase them. They run. Everyone's a bit afraid of Dick Grub.

Then he is moving on again. Back to Duxton? Or is it another village or farm he knows of? He looks at everything in a different way from the rest of us. He sees opportunities and gleanings everywhere but nobody understands him. The police think him a thief who'll knock you down. He's been arrested many times after there was a mugging, a theft or bit of violence in Duxton. That's when they can find him – because he's a 'no fixed abode' kind of chap. They always release him afterwards. There's no evidence you see. And so he's on his way again grubbing as he may. But first he must go past the great and good that live in Kings Hall.

Kings Hall looks pristine today. All the lawns are immaculate. The trees and hedges are in good order too. The paintwork all looking nice as well, to set it off. What a large house! Why, the stable building, now garages, must be a full hundred yards away at least from the imposing front elevation. The garage block alone would serve as a small hotel! That car outside looks impressive. It's a Bentley, poised ready for a luncheon out today. A lunch with the Alderman, and Councillor Jeffs down in the town.

But who is that at one of the upper windows? Why, I do believe it's Big Bad Jim himself, and that looks like the shaven bullet head of Monkey Boy looking out too. They've got the lower casement pushed up. Now why's that? It's a damp and misty morning. Surely they don't need the air? Ah, I see. Monkey Boy is sitting there with his powerful air rifle pointing out of the window. He must be doing a bit of target practice. Very commendable! Yes, Big Bad Jim is pointing with his cane towards the front wall. Crack! That's a nice rifle that is, Monkey Boy. I heard that you use it for ratting in the far barns on your fields. When you do that you put a bit of Vaseline in the back of the pellets to kill 'em. Good idea. What? Ah, there's no time for Vaseline today. Crack! Big Jim points again. Crack! Ha, ha! Good sport this morning sir! Big Bad Jim is wearing his cruel smile.

Where's your target Monkey Boy? Oh I see! It's none other than old Dirty Dick, that garden pest himself sauntering past the front wall. Crack, crack! – And he's walking faster *now*! Good way to get rid of garden pests, this! The pellets are zinging off old Dick Grub's back, though. It's a pity, isn't it, that he's got that new looking thick coat on today to protect himself? Crack! Ah, that was better – stung his leg that time. Crack again! Oh, hit the hand now Big Jim! Yes, there's some blood. Big Bad Jim smiles again. Fine shot sir! Crack! Now you've hit his face – Dick's holding his cheek! Nice accuracy! Yes, blood there, too. Good shooting sir! Dick's hobbling off as quick as he can now. Ha ha! Big Bad Jim and Monkey Boy are happy with that. They are having a bit of good sport this morning. Only a bit of fun. Only a laugh. Good bit of target practice getting rid of these garden pests, ay? Dick won't be back for a while! Now gentlemen, are you ready for lunch? The Bentley awaits.

Chapter Five

Kings

Later that week about lunchtime one day, there was a knock on Seef's door. Seef was pleased to see Josh standing there.

"I know you're probably busy Seef," he said. "So I called at the chippy and brought some fish and chips round – and I got two cans of ale too!" He held them out before him.

"Just what I need, Josh! And I've done enough for today!" cried Seef. They went in and sat in the lounge amongst some half unpacked boxes. There were piles of books ready to go on the shelves.

"Sorry about all this," said Seef.

"No problem," replied Josh. "You've got some good old books here," he said, picking up a hardback copy of Josephus.

"Yes," said Seef. "Though that's the modern edition that repeats the medieval mistake about Herod's death date. I think they're probably getting that right now in the newer editions."

"Ah yes.   So not 4BC for Christ's birth!   Maybe 2BC."

They sat down with a table between them and began opening up the fish and chips. They cracked open the beers.

"Mmm. This looks good! Thank you Josh – and thank you Lord," he said as he began tucking in.

"Amen. I see you've got a Hebrew dictionary there too," said Josh.

"Yes, but I'm hopeless with language really," said Seef. "I avoided them somehow in my theology degree."

"I was just recapping last night over the first five books of the Bible – the Torah – and reminded myself again about those surprising codes there. You know, we Jewish kids were taught the Torah by the Rabbi's. They've known about these things for millennia."

"What sort of thing?" said Seef, carefully removing the batter from his fish and flaking off some of the cod within. "And why should we look for 'Biblical codes', do you think?"

"It is the glory of God to conceal a thing. But it is the honour of kings to search out a matter!" said Josh with a smile.

"Well, I suppose we are kings!" laughed Seef. "So

what sort of matter can we search out?"

"I was looking at a couple of them last night, but it only works with the 'Textus Receptus' - not the Alexandrian texts," said Josh. "Some of these 'codes' involve looking at a sequence of the Hebrew text with set intervals. So for example, if you start in Genesis and in the Hebrew, and come to the first that translates to the equivalent of the English – and then count 49 more letters."

"49?"

"Yes, 49 is a significant Bible number, being 7x7. Anyway, after that first 49 you get the next letter, a further 49 you get the next and so on. You do this in Genesis and it spells out TORAH."

"Oh. TORAH – meaning the first five books – well I suppose that's quite interesting, but many people would say that's just a coincidence."

"Except you can do exactly the same thing with Exodus, every 49th letter, again, spelling out again, TORAH."

"Really? The odds of that would be pretty long for a coincidence! Does it happen to the next book, Leviticus?"

"No it doesn't! There's an apparent 'miss'. But if you

go to the next – Numbers, and try that, it spells out TORAH once again – but backwards!"

"Huh! Crazy!"

"Then you go to the next book, Deuteronomy, and the same thing happens. TORAH backwards! So in the five books of the 'TORAH', it spells out TORAH twice in the first two, kind of pointing toward Leviticus and then in the fourth and fifth books, it 'points', if you like, backwards toward Leviticus again."

"So Leviticus was a puzzle? A book of special note perhaps?"

"Yes, Leviticus is seen by the Jews as God's guidebook for His newly redeemed people. And then they found on closer inspection that the same system did work, but it had to be every seventh letter instead, and it made a different word. A different word for the book for which the Hebrew title is 'Wayyiqra,' meaning 'And He Called' – a priestly guide about fellowship with God through sacrifice. Christians see that sacrifice as Christ; that is His blood, the only thing that makes us holy. As it says in Leviticus, 'You shall be holy, for I the Lord your God am holy.'"

"Well, what was the word revealed by every seventh letter?"

"What you perhaps might have expected – the Hebrew word for God 'Yahweh.' So you have the five books of the TORAH acting as double book ends pointing forward and back – to 'Yahweh'. In other words the TORAH points to Yahweh; God; and the blood of Christ I believe."

"That is astonishing," said Seef. "The odds of anything like that happening by chance must surely be zero!"

"Yes."

There was a heavy bang on the door. Seef put down his piece of fish and went. It was the police inspector.

"Hello officer."

"I was just passing Mr. Able, and I wanted to update you on our progress sir."

"Ah, you've made progress then?" said Seef.

"Well, er, not exactly physical progress as such, but we have recorded all the details onto the computer and entered it into the national and international system. We're fully plugged into all Europe and Interpol!" he replied excitedly with a grin.

"Oh. What does that do?"

"Well it means that the details of the crime are known nationally as well as internationally and any details we have, such as DNA, can be fed in to see if there's a match anywhere."

"Do you have any DNA?"

"Well no, but if we did have, it could be fed in to the computer, and meantime any *similar* crimes that occur with similar characteristics can be identified."

"So it means if someone else is murdered and their pet sheep is also killed you would see that and it would match it. I see." Seef was not especially impressed. In fact he was rather irritated that they hadn't done more. Arrested someone or something. Someone like Big Jim, Monkey Boy, or that horrible Dick Grub character who is sometimes seen around here, scrounging and carrying a garden tool. Seef decided it would be better not to voice his irritation too much, but there's one thing he had thought of that he could ask the police.

"Have you checked for suspects in the village itself inspector?"

"Well is there anyone who had been acting suspiciously sir?"

"I have heard that someone in the village has fire arms and uses them."

"Oh yes sir?"

"It's that Bully Boy Monkey Man character,

whatever his name is, who lives in the big house. And then there's his father who wields that walking stick about. That could be checked for blood. And his son..."

"Yes sir?"

"Well, he's a bodyguard who gets in fights, doesn't he? Some people think he's a bit vicious looking and that he's a bit aggressive. And he has *guns*, officer."

"We have previously checked at Kings Hall sir, and he is fully licensed to have his guns. They are kept in a secure lockable cabinet, locked at all times unless in use, and an inspection has been carried out within the last 12 months. He only uses his air rifle a bit. I believe mainly for garden pests."

"Yes but he may have used other guns you see. Has anybody checked to see if they've been fired recently? And *did* you actually check my father's body for bullets?"

"Well sir. I'm not aware. I can't be certain."

"Can't be certain? Isn't it simple enough to check?"

"Well there is a different department working on aspects of this case, we have many different officers working on it sir."

"Well that's something." Seef paused. "I'm sorry if I sounded critical. It's all been very distressing."

"I'm certain it has sir, but if I might say so sir, you are bearing up very well under the circumstances."

"Did you check the sheep before you buried it?" cried Seef.

"The sheep?"

"Yes the sheep. To find out how the sheep died!"

"Well that *is* certainly a point - food for thought sir. I'll pass all this on." The policeman paused, looking over Seef's shoulder.

"I say, is that fish and chips I can smell?" said the officer.

"It is. Would you like some? Mine's only getting cold in there."

"No I can't really on duty sir! But I think I might call and get some tonight. The missus is rather fond of 'em if you get my meaning." He made as if to leave.

"Well thank you for calling constable – I mean inspector."

Seef went to close the door before he might go and say something he'd really regret later. The policeman on Seef's doorstep turned to go.

"No trouble sir, and you can now rest assured that we are 'on the job' as it were."

Seef managed to control himself.

"Mmm, well goodbye for now then."

He could easily have exploded in irritation. A killer loose, and all they could do was tap away at a computer. He thought they ought at least to be out on the beat asking questions or something. Fish and chips indeed! He closed the door and went back to Josh.

"I'm not convinced by the way the police go about things," he said. "But never mind that; I wanted to ask you about the reading and the sermon last Sunday."

"The sermon was appropriate," said Josh, "and the reading reminded me of my Jewish studies."

"Really?" said Seef. "Though the first part of the reading made me think. I thought it was a bit too much with the begat type things at the end. And all from the King James with the thee's and ye's. Yes, and the sermon. Ha! I've just realised why I'm angry – because my father's murderer is still loose! That makes my countenance fall all right! But I just didn't think it worked reading the genealogy, did you?"

"Well it gives some genealogy there in that chapter, but it really gets interesting in the next chapter, chapter 5."

"Do you think so? I glanced at that in the pew Bible and it looked like more of the same 'begats'. I thought it was all a bit boring."

"Often," said Josh, "God has put something important in obscure places. If you ever see something difficult it's always worth seeking it out in the Bible. Though it has 66 books and was written by perhaps 40 or 50 different people over two thousand years – it represents, I believe, an integrated message system from beyond our time constraints and forms, a co-ordinated whole, even though the writers themselves clearly didn't set out to co-operate in that way. It's supernatural! And don't be put off by the King James, Seef. They've been trying to change to a modern version here in Kings Sternton, but one or two of us have been resisting that."

"But aren't the new versions more accurate translations and based on the oldest texts?"

"They are *thought* to be accurate translations, but the Alexandrian texts are not the best. And it was a case where the oldest didn't mean best. The KJV actually has the oldest backing text now. The 'Textus Receptus', on which the King James is based, has easily the *most* Greek and more Hebrew 'original copies' by far. It's just that there weren't any really old Textus Receptus texts found until recently. And it seems that the Alexandrian people took some liberties with their own 'T.R.' There is

72

evidence that they marked words and verses that they then removed from their version, making it about 7-10% smaller. It does affect doctrine too. And, you know, the *oldest* fragment of Matthew (in Magdalen College, Oxford) has been dated to 60 AD - and it backs up the King James - not the NIV."

"Ah! Alexandria and Origen, I suppose. But the thee's and ye's!"

"That's simple. It's singular if it starts with 'T', plural if it starts with 'Y'. The original Greek has that distinction, which we don't have in modern English. So it's easy – and more precise – when you get used to it. Scripture says that God *preserved* His word and the more you look at it, the more you realise He has. You then ask where exactly. It seems the Authorized is the best candidate."

"So throw the other versions away?"

"No, they're useful. They're good as commentaries and to aid understanding - so that I think the Lord did also oversee them and He uses them. But the accuracy of the KJV shows that it *is* God's word. It is amazing that we can actually hold it in our hands, that is this Word of God in English, you know."

"But I can't believe modern biblical scholars would have got misled, as you suggest."

"The big change in Bible translation came in 1881 when two rather dubious translators by the names of Westcott and Hort published a new Greek Bible based on the Alexandrian texts, mainly the Sinaiticus – which were said to be the oldest 'complete' Bible copies. They had survived, they said, because they were on vellum rather than parchment like the Textus Receptus used. Vellum lasts longer. Remember everything we have is *copies*. We don't have real 'originals'. They say all this about modern biblical translation because it's the party line. But all the new versions are slightly different and contain mistakes."

"I've heard that said and I've said it too," put in Seef, "when someone has asked me about which version is inerrant and infallible. The standard reply is, 'It is infallible in the original Greek.' I hadn't considered that we haven't got the original – only copies – and I certainly didn't query whether those copies were corrupt! But how can we find out which copies were corrupt and which is the 'infallible word' which is not corrupt?" asked Seef.

Josh suddenly got up, went to the hall door and listened.

"You okay?" asked Seef.

"Sorry," replied Josh, "I thought I heard something. A clue. Yes, it was."

"Maybe the police are digging in the garden!"

"I think not. But anyway, Bible translations need research."

"Oh?"

"It's also detective work," said Josh. "There are clues if you look into it closely. Like with any crime, if you don't bother to look and investigate carefully, then you are more likely to follow your fanciful suspicions and emotions – and your biases – and get it wrong." He stared hard at Seef, but Seef himself didn't seem to take the hint or to make the connection with the murder and his own ideas about suspects.

"What sort of detectives work on the texts?" asked Seef.

"The Textus Receptus is in 'Koine' Greek, which everyone agreed was the original in upper and lower case with gaps. I maintain the T.R. is how the Word of God came to us. The Alexandrian texts are in UNCIAL Greek, which is all in capitals with no gaps. But - and here is a clue coming - there are gaps in the lines and on their pages where certain passages were left out. Why would they have gaps at the very places the Textus Receptus gives the full version? So if you went to the place of a crime and you saw something odd, or you thought something was missing, wouldn't you want to investigate?" Again Josh looked very hard at Seef.

But Seef didn't get the hint again; he was thinking about Greek.

"So Westcott and Hort produced something even worse - from corrupted copies?"

"Yes, they tried to imitate the older type Koine Greek and that has wound up in the Nestles edition of the Greek New Testament. But these two men were not sympathetic to the gospel. Hort thought evangelicals were 'perverted'. Westcott thought Jesus was not God. Just consider their version. The 'Lord Jesus Christ' is omitted many times in favour of merely 'Jesus' or 'the One'. They omit several texts that show that Jesus is God or when the New Testament refers to the Trinity.

"Since Westcott and Hort didn't believe in the atonement, the words 'blood' and 'sacrifice' were omitted in one or two places as well – not everywhere – but of course it slightly weakens the message. There's a pattern to it. Does it matter? You decide. You remember what it says in the Old Testament, which hasn't been corrupted so much. The 'blood cries out' (that was from our reading in church recently)."

Yet *again* Josh looked across at Seef, but Seef's mind was still on the text corruptions Josh had mentioned. Oh, Seef, wake up!

"Give me some actual examples," said Seef.

"In Acts 8, the Ethiopian (after 'conversion') says to Philip, 'What doth hinder me to be baptised?' Verse 37 in the KJV says that Philip replies, 'If thou believest with all thine heart thou mayest.' And the Ethiopian answered and said, 'I believe that Jesus Christ is the Son of God.' The Ethiopian then commanded the chariot to stand still and they go to the water. In the NIV, it misses out verse 37 completely and we get, 'What can stand in the way of my being baptised? And he gave orders to stop and they go to the water.' Believing with all your heart and belief that Jesus Christ is the Son of God omitted! Sometimes the new versions have a mere footnote for a place like that. They say, 'some manuscripts have this, but the best and the oldest manuscripts don't have it.' They are not correct in saying, 'the best and the oldest.' And it weakens the message again, you see."

Josh continued, "Colossians 1:13,14 says, 'He has delivered us from the power of darkness, and hath translated us into the Kingdom of his dear Son, in whom we have redemption *through his blood*, even for the forgiveness of sins.' Seef, do you think the blood is important?"

"Absolutely, it is impossible to overstate it."

"Of course, anybody's blood is life itself. Think about that Seef. And the blood of Jesus is redemption for sinners. The NIV misses out the words, 'through his blood', however! It's elsewhere in Scripture, so does it matter? I think it does, but anyway I don't particularly want some unbelievers like Westcott and Hort tinkering about with my Bible before I get it."

"Absolutely – but why would they do that?"

"Is it because they, being more influenced by the enemy than God, are trying to water down the heart of the gospel? Seef, if you heard of a murder case where they ignored what they had heard about the blood and they saw, say a murder weapon, that was missing from its place, what would you think of them if they ignored these things?" Josh gave Seef the same hard look.

"I would say these translators are falling down on the job, or deliberately trying to pull the wool over someone's eyes."

Josh nodded, but also sighed.

"Yes! I can see it!" cried Seef.

Josh's eyes lit up.

"These Alexandrian Gnostics and these Victorian, liberal and unbelieving translators were used by Satan to water down faith and fool us with a corrupt version!"

Josh smiled and nodded again. Yes and yes - but once more he was a little disappointed. He had hoped Seef would get two enlightenings at once, about the Bible and the murder; but Josh was expecting too much of poor Seef.

"But really Seef, *why* do we want liberals changing things to suit their own preferences and agenda?" asked Josh. "I would prefer the pure word! So *who* do you think would want to remove these references? Who do you think would want to put you on the wrong track by watering down and effectively spinning a web of deceit?" Josh looked quizzingly at Seef.

"The enemy?"

"Yes, the enemy. A supernatural enemy. Do you wonder what God might have done? Do you not think

He could have *preserved* His word against supernatural enemies?"

Chapter Six

Preserved Words

"Of course supernatural enemies use people on earth to help them," said Josh. "There's another story I could tell. It actually concerns a possible murder, or at the least a very strange disappearance."

"Go on," said Seef.

"There was a young man who lived in Greece in the 1800s. I'll call him Simon. He was skilled at copying old Bible texts. His uncle, a monastery abbot, wanted a facsimile - a parchment copy - of the Bible done with old style lettering as a gift to the Czar of Russia. Simon had nearly completed it when his uncle died. He finished it hastily and asked his uncle's friends what he should do with it. They suggested not giving it to the Czar, but instead giving it to a monastery in the desert, where visitors could look at it as a curiosity and perhaps make a contribution to monastery funds. This Simon did.

"Years pass. Along to the desert monastery comes Friedrich, a famous Biblical scholar. He mistakes Simon's work for an ancient Bible. Somehow he doesn't think about how white the sheets are, which would indicate newness. Now Friedrich is a rather roguish opportunist. He steals a small part of it from the monastery hoping it won't be noticed. He takes it home, has it published, and Friedrich is acclaimed for his discovery! However, the monks *do* notice that part is missing, and complain, but no-one listens to them. They decide to hide the rest of it away.

"Further time passes. Friedrich wants some more, so back he goes! At first he can't find the remaining parchments, but then he tricks the monk who has it and manages to steal the rest of it. However, once he gets it away and looks at it carefully, he realises it is only a modern facsimile! He is very cross, but because he has already said the other part was genuine, he decides he will have no alternative but to try to pass off the other part he stole as genuine too.

"He stains it with lemon juice to make the parchment look old. He alters it quite a bit to match a similar codex in the Vatican. He takes bits out and removes a page or so. He 'liberalises' it a bit. He will make sure it is kept in a different city far away from the first sheets that he stole, so that they won't be compared for colour. So he then publishes the new part he has - again to great acclaim. He is even more famous! But then, much to Friedrich's alarm, the man who made it -

Simon himself turns up, and looks at what has been published! He examines the work, saying it is the very same pages that he wrote out years before, and he produces proofs, and also says how he made certain marks of his own on the parchment! And then someone else says they saw Friedrich with the lemon juice! Simon challenges Friedrich to a debate to prove it is his and to examine the document. Friedrich initially says yes - but then he doesn't show up. Shortly after that - get this! - Simon completely disappears! Some say he died somewhere in Russia or Egypt; some say he was murdered. We don't know for sure.

"Some murders happen when people grow irritated with someone, and end up lashing out when sin comes to the door. Then the blood cries out to God. And he *may* reveal it to us, Seef. Meantime, Friedrich manages to convince people that Simon was a fraud, and enjoys the fruits of his cunning deception. He claimed, as bold as brass, that it was the oldest Bible in existence."

"Sounds like the Friedrich in your story had a lot to answer for," remarked Seef.

"But yes, after the initial questions, as I said, he pretty well got away with it," said Josh. "Now, what if I told you this was a true story and these were real people, and that the deception had worked right up to the present day?"

"That would be pretty shocking."

"Simon's full name was Simonides, a Greek scribe, and once a Greek war hero. Friedrich was Constantin Friedrich von Tischendorf - who is still acclaimed as the 'discoverer' of the Greek 'Textus Sinaiticus' - which he claimed he found chucked in a waste paper bin in the Sinai monastery! The monks had told a different story of how it was stolen, but they weren't listened to or believed."

"'Textus Sinaiticus' rings a bell. From Alexandria I think you said earlier?" Seef asked.

"Yes, and that is the text on which *all* the modern versions of the Bible are based, rather than the 'Textus Receptus', which was used for the KJV."

"Now that too *is* shocking!"

"The 'Sinaiticus' suited the Liberal Theologians, being a garbled and altered version that they could argue their interpretations about, and with the missing bits some of the doctrines could be watered down. But these sheets, which have been carefully photographed, can of course *now* be compared on the internet to expose the fraud. The first lot is pure white, the second lot yellowish! They should be identical. So all the modern Bible versions are based on Friedrich's garbled fraud - the 'Textus Sinaiticus'. (That and the 'Textus Vaticanus' - a dubious and modernish Vatican document that Friedrich had referred to.) But Psalm 12 says that God would *preserve* His word, and I think He did, in the Antioch 'Textus Receptus', which comes down to us in English in the KJV."

"I suppose the other Egyptian versions were never-the-less kept okay by God in *some* sense?"

"Yes, I think so. But our loving God said He would preserve His word. However, because He does want to tell us things clearly, He has watched over it over the centuries all through the copying and distribution process right up until today. His word is a revelation in a pattern that He has kept intact. God works with specific, accurate words, numbers and patterns. Thus in your case, with the mystery you are trying to solve, you might care to notice a pattern. If the pattern crops up again, in any revelation Seef – you might watch for it – God could be giving you a message!" (But Josh's advice about how to solve the murder weren't working.)

"Me – a message? Huh! But wait Josh! Everyone knows the KJV is full of errors!"

"They usually say that because they think the Egyptian texts are older, which I've just explained is a problem. And further research explains these so-called 'errors'. Where would you rather get your Bible from - Egypt or Antioch?"

"We usually associate Egypt with error and Antioch with the first 'Christians'."

"Yes."

"But I suppose with the Bible the early church *did* have the originals, didn't they?" asked Seef.

"I'll quote something from 2 Timothy," said Josh.

'From a child thou [Timothy] hast known the Holy Scriptures, which are able to make thee wise unto salvation through faith which is in Christ Jesus. All Scripture is given by inspiration of God... That the man of God may be perfect.'

"Of course the very originals did exist. But this reference in Timothy may *not* be a reference to original manuscripts", Josh continued, "but to careful *copies* of the original. The Bible, you know, probably always talks of *copies* in this context. It doesn't say anywhere 'find the originals'. It is *God* Himself who preserved His Word in *copies* to this time! The prophetic words and *patterns* of God in the Bible are still maintained, and prophecies and teachings are often repeated. This is helpful when you're studying, say, end times.

"God certainly does preserve as well as inspire. See Psalm 12:6 and 7, 'The words of the Lord are pure... Thou shalt keep them, O Lord, Thou shalt preserve them from this generation for ever'. And Matthew 5:18 says, 'Till heaven and earth pass, one jot or one tittle shall in no wise pass from the law (the Scriptures we could say), till all be fulfilled.' (The law is really fulfilled for us in Christ, as you know. Luke 4:4 says, 'Man shall not live by bread alone, but by every word of God.' So we can't just have odd words removed! The purpose of the Textus Receptus was to providentially preserve the infallibility of the divine text and it came from the first Christians in Antioch in Syria. That was the word of God then, which we now have as the KJV!"

"Mmm, I suppose when you pull all the Scriptures together, you can see that," said Seef. "That reading the other day... Now there's something ringing around in the back of my mind... the blood speaks... the word speaks."

"Yes?" said Josh eagerly looking at Seef.

"Oh nothing. It will come to be later I expect. It's just amazing that we can say we have the word of God – which leads us to Jesus – The Word made flesh."

"Yes, study the written word too, Seef. Everything will come to you. The word is so important. Psalm 138:2 says, 'for thou hast magnified thy word above all thy name'. Above thy name, Seef! Christians need to ask themselves where such a word 'above His name' is found."

"True. And I was just thinking of that other Scripture too."

"Which?"

"2 Corinthians 2:17: 'For we are not as many, which corrupt the word of God'. Many have corrupted it, apparently!"

"Good point, and it's worth remembering again, Seef, that it's a *supernatural* book. It talks about, prophesies and gives pictures for events that will or may happen thousands of years into the future.

"When we study the Bible in detail we'll realise it *is* prophetic and reveals truths that *cannot* have been known at the time it was written," continued Josh. "I would say that the more detailed our studies, the more useful we'll find the KJV. It has the precision we should expect from the word that God has preserved. If there is such a miraculous word, it should be without errors. Like I said, it's a supernatural communication system coming to us from outside our time frame and natural reference points. And it even has messages and truth hidden inside!"

"As you explained with the code in Hebrew letters you mean? But anyway, what did you see in the genealogy in Genesis, chapter 5?" asked Seef.

"A message, which it was the glory of God to hide, waiting for us kings to seek out! The Bible has much more than number codes. Much more. Prophetic passages are sometimes fulfilled or partially fulfilled later – on many levels – right up to and including modern times – and certain phrases and lines often take place right down to the personal events in people's lives today!" Josh looked at Seef. "Information and prophecy all linked and sometimes semi-hidden. Now in Genesis chapter 5 – once more, if again you go back to the Hebrew you have in that genealogy a total of ten people's names. It's actually the meanings of these names which are important. So for example you have Methuselah amongst them which means 'His death shall bring.'"

"Methuselah! That reminds me," cried Seef, "of a puzzle joke someone told me. He asked, 'Who was the oldest man in the Bible?' Of course I answered 'Methuselah,' but he said, 'No, his father, Enoch, was born before him and hadn't yet died when Methuselah died.' A kind of a trick question! I was forgetting Enoch was 'taken' and never died."

"True! Yes, so as I said, Methuselah's name means in Hebrew, 'His death shall bring.' Methuselah's father, Enoch, was given a prophecy that when his son died judgement would come upon the earth by a great flood. Sure enough, Methuselah died in the very year before the flood, at 969 years old! Anyway, to get back to the genealogy in Genesis 5. You get this list of names, which begins with Adam, which simply means 'man', and his son was named your name, Seth, which means 'appointed'."

"Ah that's me!" cried Seef, "I get appointed to do this and that. Usually difficult building problems. That's been my life! Appointed to do hard things!"

"Sometimes they are too hard for you, Seef! Anyway, Seth's son was Enosh which means 'mortal' and Enosh's son was Cainan which means 'sorrow'. Then comes Mahalalel which means 'the blessed God.'

"I suppose these all had significant meanings for all their individual lives at that time?"

"Oh yes. And then the next in the list was Jared, meaning 'shall come down'. His son was Enoch himself and his name means 'teaching'.

"Well he *was* an esteemed prophet and teacher I believe. People followed him around, that is, until he was 'taken.'"

"A type of the Rapture! Enoch was or we should say *is* a holy man. I told you what his son Methuselah's name means. Methuselah's own son was Lamech which means 'the despairing'."

"Imagine being called despairing!"

"His son was Noah, which means 'comfort' or 'rest'."

"I see," said Seef. "Yes I can see it's interesting with these meanings applying to their lives."

"It gets even more interesting when you put them together."

"What? How d'you mean?"

"Well, if you set just the *meanings* of the names down in the same biblical order..."

"You get?"

"Man (is) appointed mortal sorrow; the blessed God shall come down, teaching His death shall bring the

91

despairing comfort (and) rest."

Seef stared at Josh open mouthed, and didn't speak for a moment.

"Now that is astonishing!" he cried at last. "A prophetic utterance about Jesus Christ crucified and His salvation embedded right there in the genealogy of names in Genesis 5. And in a passage I said we should skip over and not even read. Incredible!"

"You never know what's in the Bible text," said Josh quietly. "That's why it's always worth extra study. You never get to the bottom with Scripture. But now I have to go, Seef."

They got up and walked into the hall.

"Trouble with the floor boards?" asked Josh, looking at the mess.

"Yes, amongst other things! I'm planning to get some help for all this."

"Is it all right beneath the boards?" asked Josh.

"Probably not, I have to investigate it."

"I should," said Josh. "There's a noise coming from beneath there. It may help guide you with your investigations."

"Mmm, don't know I've heard much, or maybe I have. Not sure," said Seef, "but then I sometimes wonder if my hearing's the best. What sort of noise?"

"It's a trickling kind of sound. I should investigate it carefully if I were you."

"Ah yes! I thought I'd dreamt it. But I will now you've said," replied Seef. "I was half tempted to just board it over."

"No, it's worth a look," said Josh. "Anyway I'll see you – probably on Sunday."

Seef let him out. "Thanks for the fish and chips!" he cried. "That was welcome." Josh smiled back and waved as he walked towards the gate.

Chapter Seven

A Wanderer and a Vagabond on Earth

It was a little later than he had intended when Seef finally got to call on Jez. He walked round to her house, which of course was only just next door. As he walked up her path, he couldn't help noticing how poor the garden looked. There were lots of dead and dying plants and those that were alive looked shrivelled. At the front door he paused, looking at the house sign. It was in pastel colours and it said 'Noddy's Land' with a picture of the boy himself. It seemed inappropriate. (Seef should have thought about it!) Next he looked at the knocker. It was some kind of ceramic material with a single eye in the middle. It looked rather evil. It reminded him of the design on the dollar bill. He rapped on the door with it.

He heard a distant female voice shout, 'Wait' and after a minute Jez appeared. When he saw her his first thought was that he shouldn't have come. He felt she looked a little displeased.

"Hello Seef. Where have you been? And what have you done to my potatoes?" The scar on her forehead looked as if it had swollen and looked especially menacing he thought.

"Your potatoes?"

"In the garden. They've all died."

"Oh that's a pity."

"You haven't been spraying weed killer over the fence then? Only some people do that to their neighbours, you know."

"Certainly not. In any case I don't like those weed killer sprays – they make me cough. And it would be no good for the lamb you see."

"Ah yes the lamb. By the way, I'd rather you didn't cross my corner but instead go round the Green Lane way. I know it's further but you're a fit chap!"

"Ok – as you've asked – though there is a right of way – anyway I came about the tap and..."

"Oh yes, of course. I've got another guest here besides Lily, but that's alright."

"I can come at another time."

"No! Today's fine. Well I know you're busy and everything."

"Yes I've got a lot to do, I wasn't sure I could make it, but I did say that I would."

"Seef, you are a rascal, you know!" she said, "I was expecting you before this." She was trying to lighten up, realising she must have sounded severe at first.

"Well I've come to look at the tap and..."

"Ok." She beckoned him in. "Yes, if you knew the trouble we have with that tap!"

They stood in her hall.

"Oh! Unusual decoration you have!"

"Yes, it is unusual."

Seef looked around at the dark grey walls. The banisters had been picked out in pink, and there were also pink panels on the walls. Inside the panels were various objects that were fixed there, such as horsewhips, leather belts and buckles, and pictures of leather-clad women wielding them. He also noticed a thumbscrew.

"Yes," she said noticing his look. "It's been a passion of mine to collect instruments of torture – purely for fun of course! But I wouldn't mind getting the person who killed my potatoes in one of those." She pointed at the thumbscrew.

"It's probably just potato blight," said Seef. "These things happen."

"Yes but it's so upsetting," she cried. "After all our work. It gets me angry and down sometimes. Makes me cross," she added. Her scar seemed to be getting redder as she spoke.

"Ah well, if we follow the advice in the sermon on Sunday, we'll just try to do the best we can with God's help and not let it trouble us like that."

"Pooh-pooh. That's all very well. But we live in a stressful world, and I've got a fool of a husband, too."

"But I do think God can help with today's issues. I find He does with me when I ask Him." said Seef.

"Forget it. I'll just get the plough out sometime and plough it all up and start again," said Jez.

"Ah yes," said Seef. "I noticed the plough down there. It looked as if something was missing from it and needed fixing."

"Well, I'd better show you this tap," she said, turning quickly back to the stairs.

"Hey, Floozy! Lily!" she cried. "There's a *man* in the hall coming upstairs."

There were a couple of short yelps heard from above, and Seef followed Jez upstairs. The tiles in the bathroom were black.

"I didn't mean to disturb you like this," said Seef.

"Don't worry. Lily lodges and I often have another girlfriend here to stay." She winked.

Seef looked at the tap. He'd brought his screwdriver,

so he undid the top, unscrewed it below to get to the washer and then took it out and turned the washer completely around and put it back in. He then screwed it all back on, and put the top of the tap on again. He tried it. It worked, and it didn't drip.

"That should be okay now."

"What, is that *it*?"

"Well I've done it temporarily. But it should last for months. If you ever get a plumber here for anything else, you can tell him to replace it properly."

"Oh! Well thanks. I thought it would be major. Anyway, I expect I'll see you at St. Do Dahs on Sunday."

"Yes it seems quite good there. Mrs Welch might be getting me a bacon sandwich next week! I liked the reading and the sermon the vicar gave."

"Pooh. And Mrs Welch is a gossipy old goat, and the vicar wench is too much of a Bible thumper! She's not assertive enough for feminist causes! The place is a bit old fashioned, to be honest, but I feel I *have* to support them. And I do quite a lot of visiting with my particular interests promoting liberation of sexuality expression and galloping around in connection with a report I'm doing for the Diocese. I'm a wanderer and a vagabond on the face of the earth you know."

"Oh."

"Yes, I'm also in charge of a team that does educational reports. At the moment it's on the LGBTQ+ position with regard to transgender equality in the schools. The last one was on equality in marriage. Once we report, the bishops take our findings to synod and will push it through like I tell 'em to. We've got to get the church into the 21st Century, the poor old dear."

"Indeed! You think so? Ah well. I must be going. See you soon I suppose." She let him out and Seef walked quickly back along the garden path. He'd forgotten about the cracked glass in Jez' conservatory, but he had no intention of going back there if he could possibly help it.

Chapter Eight

The Law

A few weeks passed. A few weeks of no progress on the murder enquiry. A few weeks when Seef had been working away on the house but frustrated by his own lack of progress. There had been too many interruptions. Sometimes he just felt too tired and had to walk away from it. Today was one of those days like that. And it had been raining. That was why Seef was visiting at Josh's cottage today.

They got deep into conversation. Josh first asked him if he'd had any moments of remembrance or revelations since their last conversation about the King James Bible, or even from looking over apocryphal works like the Book of Jasher, which was worth reading, he said, for 'edification'.

"No," said Seef, "but then I'm not much good at remembering what it was I was even trying to remember in the first place!"

"I see! Do you find it easy to remember *Bible verses*? asked Josh.

"From the traditional version - it's easier."

"I think it's because the King James uses Anglo Saxon one syllable words, where the newer versions use Latinised words of several syllables. Also, as a society, we've moved from a word-based culture to an *image* based one. But I've found in some of my work with children that they too can remember the old version better than the modern ones. Maybe God played His part in the process and preserves it in people's minds because it's His word – and it could be the opposite too – a *loss* of speech if it's not His word."

"How do you mean?"

"Well I did actually hear that some of the liberalising editors of the new versions actually lost their ability to speak for a time."

"Really!"

"Yes, and sometimes it was actually taped on TV! It happened in the Bible, you remember, when someone didn't believe John the Baptist's father..."

"He lost his voice!"

"And then Paul lost his sight. He had set his eye on mischief at Damascus by killing Christians, so the Holy Spirit blinded him. At that moment when he sees the light, Paul knows it is God, so he says, 'Lord, who are you?' When he is told it is Jesus, he then calls Jesus,

'Lord', so we know he is converted to Christ at that moment. The later versions don't record Paul's reply; because maybe they didn't want Jesus to be called Lord more than was strictly necessary! Now modern translators have indeed woken up to the problem of these omissions, because of complaints, and are starting to add back in some of the Textus Receptus. The latest Nestles Greek, has added back in 480 words.

"Anyway," continued Josh, "you said you haven't remembered what you wanted to, Seef; I just wondered also if you'd had a look under the hall floor yet?"

"No, but I have been checking out a few people who might be suspects – vagrants, or people with guns – that kind of thing."

Josh sighed gently, then he said, "When we had that reading the other day in church, it was striking about the blood, and then I mentioned, didn't I, about their leaving out about the blood in the newer versions."

"What Josh? Sorry, I was looking at your shofar on the wall. That's what we'll hear at the rapture!"

"Indeed! But I wonder Seef; do you think blood cries out?"

"I'm not sure; the Bible says it somewhere. There's something about blood on their hands. Where did you get your shofar?"

Josh realised Seef wasn't going to respond to his prompting, so he decided to change the subject.

"Israel. Have you been?"

"I've seen the tourist sites."

"It's interesting," said Josh, "that the tourist guides all use the Bible as a guide book when they are taking you around the Holy Land. Did you notice that?"

"As a matter of fact I did," Seef replied. "These were secular guides too." Seef paused. "I don't always know what to make of Israel. I mean it's wonderful what they've done there, turning the desert into an oasis, and there are obviously a lot of the main monotheistic religions all being openly practised in some parts of the country, yet there are other parts, like Tel Aviv, where it all seems very secular."

Josh nodded and began explaining and telling him about the role of Israel in the last days. He said that many, even in the church, didn't understand or know this at all. Many Christians mistakenly believed in 'replacement theology'. This is where the church has replaced Israel. But God *has* a plan – and it is shown in

103

the Bible. The actual nation of Israel is still 'God's chosen people', but gets picked on by the world. None of her neighbours (There are now a couple of exceptions.) want her to even exist. They want to push her into the sea! Yet she is the only true democracy in the Middle East. She is a green jewel in the desert, a place of learning and innovation, a world leader in many fields, and a place where the Arabs living there can find peace and employment.

Josh continued explaining that the Palestinians – who never were a state before – now want to *be* a state on her piece of ground. And the dusty desert lands all around, where the Muslims live, also *want* her tiny bit of land. They deny she has any right to be there! They even deny all her history as set out in the Bible. They say it's lies, and Jews were never there! They attack her citizens. They plant bombs on buses. They send over rockets. They stab Israelis in the streets. They demonstrate and try to shut down Israeli institutions and disable them. They organise the left wing liberals in the universities in the west to campaign against her!

Recently they organised a 'black list' of Israeli companies operating in the West Bank. The UN – who are biased in favour of the Palestinians – have been trying to publish it. The idea is to get shareholders to abandon Israeli companies. They use false propaganda and lies to make her sound terrible. They get the UN to condemn her in resolutions. Scores of these resolutions (70 odd so far) have been issued, all *against* Israel. This compares with hardly any resolutions against the vilest of the world's regimes; all the other terrible abuses all around the world! Like hundreds of thousands being killed in a devastating six year civil war next door – yet nothing said by the UN! And yet she is the *only* country they condemn – a real democracy, where even Arabs sit in the Israeli parliament – and it is in the middle of a sea of non-democratic countries, with corrupt dictatorships and the like; where, amongst other things, free speech is not upheld and women's rights are ignored.

Josh shared this while Seef listened. He was rather shocked, and he decided to himself that he would definitely pray for the peace of Jerusalem.

He then heard about the holocaust deniers – a position which seemed ridiculous and incredible to Seef – and he also heard about the Jew hatred re-emerging in other places. He had no idea there was so much anti-Semitism coming out again. Our so called 'free' press didn't tell him. He'd been getting fake news.

But then there was a tap at Josh's cottage door. Josh went out to the hallway and opened the front door. Seef couldn't help listening from the front room. It was the police! For a few minutes Seef thought they were there calling for him. Had they made some progress at last and found the killer? It's high time they had got somewhere and had done something!

They were still talking to Josh at the front door. Seef stood up and stepped towards the window. Through the glass he saw three policemen and a dishevelled figure in handcuffs. Dick Grub! Yes, it was him! Seef suspected it all along. His father spoke of helping him, and Grub must have turned violently on his dad that day. Seef had thought he *ought* to be chief suspect for the murder! Well, he looked rough enough and just the type. Perhaps they had found evidence for convicting him and were bringing him around to confront him with Seef, who they found out was at Josh's cottage that afternoon. But Seef was not called to go and meet the policemen at the door.

So he sat again and listened carefully to the conversation. At first it sounded promising, but then his hopes were dashed.

"Yes sir," a policeman was saying, "so we found

him with these tools and there's blood on this 'ere knife he was carrying. He says it's from a rabbit he killed but we're not sure. And he's wearing this jacket with a name and address on it. Our suspicion sir, is that he has stolen this stuff from your property and we need to get you to agree to press charges."

"Against my friend, Dick?" Seef heard Josh say. "No, certainly not. I *gave* him these items."

The policemen were quiet. They were in reality staring very hard at Josh. And Dick Grub, who hitherto had been glancing about him nervously, began to change his look to a rugged and nervous grin.

"In fact Dick," Seef heard Josh saying, "you forgot the other coat I said you could have and your wallet! Let me fetch them!"

Seef went to the window again and a few minutes later he saw Josh handing over what looked like a new, really expensive coat with a hood and pockets and also a wallet, which didn't look empty.

"These were the things, Dick." said Josh.

The grin on Dick's face broadened as he looked at the policemen around him. He looked as if he would burst into tears of joy. "Praise Abba," he cried. He held out his hands, indicating that, perhaps the moment had come when they could remove the handcuffs. As they did so he nodded and beamed at those around him.

"'E helped me," he said, pointing to Josh. "'E's m' friend 'e is."

"Are you sure sir?" said the officer to Josh. "This doesn't seem quite right that he's got all this 'ere stuff and that he left these items here."

"Oh yes, it's quite right," replied Josh.

In the sitting room Seef decided it would be better to return to his chair and say nothing and pretend he hadn't heard the exchange. When Josh came in, he waited for an explanation, but strangely he didn't say anything at all about it, and he simply carried on with the previous conversation.

But later on the way home, Seef found himself rather cross at what Josh had done.

"Grub probably *is* the blighter who slaughtered the sheep and poisoned Jez's potatoes as well – at least. Why he probably has done many worse things too... I don't like the look of him. I might remind the police, and even make discreet enquiries for myself."

Chapter Nine

Building Work

It had now been a couple of months since Seef had arrived in Kings Sternton and things had worked out quite differently from what he had expected. Staszek had been in touch and said he couldn't come till later. That meant that most of the big jobs had been left.

For another thing, Seef himself hadn't been feeling really fit and well over the period. He often felt tired. He hadn't been able to do anything towards the front elevation remodelling. He had acquired some of the roof timbers but found he needed most of them when he repaired Mi's roof. And his own roof repair had been more complicated than he thought and really required re-felting underneath. And it was still leaking.

Then another neighbour had noticed that he had some felt, and asked if he could 'borrow' some for his shed roof. But then he wasn't able to do it very well on his own and came back to Seef for help. And Seef found he had to use a lot of his own roofing battens to fix it down. It was rather a large shed.

Seef felt so bushed and exhausted after doing that, that he *just* had to forget it the next day. He had a day with his books. He also played patience and looked into a book of puzzles.

And then also to slow him down, Jez's husband had kept on coming round numerous times wanting to 'borrow' tools (he never saw them again), or 'pinch' a bit of his wood (which left him short for his own projects). With all this Seef found his early retirement wasn't working out anything like he imagined. But a big plus had been getting to know Josh.

Josh came around regularly and had explained many interesting things, not only from the Bible, but about the Spirit-filled life. The details would not have interested everybody, but it was exactly right for Seef. But there was more to it than that. With the talks with Josh, Seef had found his own faith and trust had increased. He even found he was able to put up with some of the inconveniences and annoyances a bit better than he had expected of himself. He speculated that as he drew closer to God, the 'fruit' which was often beyond his reach, was actually produced without any effort of his own.

Meanwhile the lack of progress on the investigation of the murder still irked him. He decided he *would* do a few enquiries himself, and he actually drove into Duxton a couple of times and walked around to see if he could find out anything about the Dick Grub character. His efforts didn't get him very far with that. He discovered the very poor and miserable life that Dick was leading. There wasn't much real evidence, but what he did hear made him more suspicious. He was also finding out more and more incriminating things about Big Jim and Monkey Boy.

Monkey Boy, it seemed, was an overgrown and spoilt bully, and Big Jim, his father, was Monkey Boy's inspiration. Big Jim had tried, Seef heard, to get most of the village and half of Duxton into his pocket. It seemed that Jim had no qualms about knocking people out of his way if they annoyed him. Seef also found out the very interesting fact that Big Jim had wanted to build some houses on his own field at the back, but the proposal was partially blocked for access by Weelike's field! And then apparently Seef's father had refused to sell his own field to him. All very interesting! Big Jim was after the land and so, if the owner proved difficult - well, he could be 'wasted'!

Anyway, meantime Seef carried on with the work on Amen House as best as he could. Then one day he suddenly remembered about the hall floor. Josh had said there was a trickling noise coming from below, so he thought it was high time he investigated.

The floor boards underneath tore up easily enough, being rotten, and many of the joists came out too. Underneath he saw that he would have to clean it right out and put in a membrane and some concrete lean mix. That afternoon he started. There were lots of stones and gravel and dusty topsoil, but among it all he found an iron bar painted dark green with blackish red marks on it. It seemed oddly familiar to him. He laid it on the hall floor, and turned back to make a note of the new materials he needed for the new under-floor, the joists and the boards on top.

That evening he ordered in an Indian curry, one of his favourites, and afterwards he sat with a sketchpad idly drawing out more detailed designs for the carving on the spandrels over the porch. These decorative touches were to be inset in the timber, and he'd gone to considerable trouble to find the right oak for them. He had found a hardwood specialist some twenty miles away, and now the pieces were lying in his barn. He had paid more for them than he had intended really. But they were a sweet wood. After he brought them back he'd spent some time sanding and admiring the grain. Beautiful! They had been cured for at least ten years and were just the ticket.

Anyway, a few days later he was still toying with the design. After sketching for a while that evening he thought he would check the width of the timber to see if the design he wanted would fit. He went outside and over to the barn and he peered around in the old building. Gone! The timber had gone! Nothing there! He looked high and low and elsewhere. Where was it? These were sizeable pieces of wood. Perhaps he had put them in the house. He started back.

But as he went he noticed Jez's husband doing something to the fence. George nodded and he waved. But something made him walk a little closer – then he saw it - the fool was nailing *his* oak to make a repair to the fence!

"Whatever are you doing?" cried Seef.

"Jez has been on about me repairing the fence here for ages. We hadn't got any wood so she said, 'well go round to Seef's and find some. He's bound to have bits of scrap.' I was going to knock, but then I saw these twisted

113

old knotty bits lying in your barn."

"Old knotty bits! These are for the spandrels of my porch! I spent ages finding them!"

"What are spandrels?"

"They're the oak decorative bits above – oh! It doesn't *matter* – this is terrible!"

"Oh!" said George. "Only decorative bits? Oak? No wonder it was so hard to cut and drill all of my holes."

"My spandrels!" exploded Seef. "You f..."

"I thought they were rubbish. They're not even straight."

"Thought they were rubbish! They're not rubbish and they're not meant to be straight. Oh – this is impossible! Now you've completely ruined them on this stupid fence."

"Well the fence is important to Jez you know. She wants it animal proof, she says. Now it's nice and strong."

"Ugh!" cried Seef and marched away before he was tempted to clobber him.

He went back to the house. This was *so* infuriating. He cried out, "Oh God help me out of this situation. I can't stand these people. They are driving me mad! And I haven't got anywhere with the enquiries about my father's killer either. Nothing is going right here, Lord. My head is throbbing. I need your help!"

He went to the medicine cupboard and got a couple of Anadins. Then he went and sat down and closed his eyes. Somehow, he realised, he must get a grip. Normally things didn't bother him but he had been so looking forward to doing the spandrels. These people next door were next to impossible. He decided to deliberately block them from his mind. Somehow he must get his mind onto something else. He opened his eyes. His Bible was lying there. Josh was always saying it was a supernatural book, with hidden messages inside for followers of Christ to find. And Josh had said there were multiple fulfilments of things that happened in the Bible; patterns that repeated again and again. And Seef believed in miracles and that God could help.

He opened it. It was *Genesis 4*, the same passage he'd heard in church when he first arrived there. It didn't seem appropriate to his situation but he read it anyway. Afterwards he decided to go and call on Mi to make himself feel better. When he got there Mi greeted him.

"Oh Mr Seef! You want fried rice? I cook for you. Come in."

"No, no. I've just eaten. I've come round because – well – I just needed a friend to talk to."

"I understand everything Mr Seef! You sit down. We chat."

They talked for a while. Seef said he'd been reading Genesis 4.

"I think it is book of Jasher says something about that Seef."

"Oh! I looked at that the other day on my laptop. I think I've still got the tab open. I'll have a read of it. I need something to distract me at present from life's agitations."

Seef then told Mi about Jez's husband taking the oak.

"I know it's not much but I feel it was the last straw with them. They're not even worthy of help either, with their stupid little jobs."

"Sometimes a small thing makes people angry and then they sin without it being their intention."

"I could have hit him."

"I understand. Your father used to get fed up with them because they came up with such minor niggles. They had a row about Weelike nibbling bits of potato tops when they crossed their land! You know it is right of way and your father had to come across *their* garden to go to the sheep and bring them back to tether them on the lawn. But even though he gave Jez a great big bag of wool that she wanted, Jez got cross. She complained so much. Once Weelike paused for too long and started eating her potato tops again. Your father said it was not much but she just went mad. That was only just before he died."

"They've blocked it now. I go round by Green Lane."

"This is your right of way across her garden for you to use."

"Well there's a great big plough in the way to make it awkward. I don't know why they have such a thing in their garden..."

Seef stopped mid-sentence. He stared at Mi. A light had just gone on.

"Something's just occurred to me," he said. "I must go and look at... something. Sorry..." He rose to go.

"Ok. Let me know what you find in Jasher. And don't let the sun go down on your anger."

But Seef had left.

Chapter Ten

Time Up

Seef raced back to his house. His mind was racing too. How could he have been so stupid when the answer to the mystery was staring him in the face? But surely God didn't work the same patterns today after thousands of years? Josh would say He does if He wants. Josh would say we can get to know His patterns and character. He went in through the front door and looked carefully at something on the hall floor. He paced about in a nervous manner. He sat down. He stood up again and walked about. Is this what revelation feels like, he wondered? 'No,' he felt he heard a voice saying, 'revelation is in many forms, but continue asking Me.'

Suddenly he got out his laptop and looked at the books of Jasher and Genesis reading them through sentence by sentence – but he did it in a kind of feverish state. He paced about. He went back to the passages and read them again. Then he strode about again for some time. He must think it through to know what to do.

The time was passing. Too late tonight! He went up to his bedroom. He would contact the police first thing in the morning. But then they needed evidence. Well, he had some of that now – surely it would help them!

He was still thinking and praying as he lay there in bed. Eventually in the small hours he started to laugh to himself. Words! That's what he should have studied. And Josh's hints. All the clues had been there from the beginning! Then he began to plan for the next day and even for doing the rest of the work on the house. Staszek was due tomorrow. They would soon make progress with all of the jobs with him there. Eventually he fell asleep. He slept very fitfully, feeling unwell.

He was woken early by a knock at the door. He hauled on his dressing gown and stumbled down the stairs feeling groggy. A man in a peaked cap stood outside. A black car was parked beyond the gate.

"Mr. Seth Able?"

"Yes."

"I'm the taxi driver to take you to the Beulah flight."

"Flight? Surely not? It can't be time already?"

"The driver glanced at a paper he was holding."

"Seth Able. Today's date, first thing this morning. Yes, it's correct."

"Oh no! Please! Not today! Please!"

"Sorry, sir. That is the arrangement, I'm afraid."

"Can I have a day or so to arrange things – my builder is coming today – or at least can I have a couple of hours? I have to see the police."

"Afraid not, sir. Five minutes is all that's allowed. You can get dressed. Grab a few things."

"Wait." Seef tore back into the house. Oh no! The very morning he had discovered the answer to the mystery that solved it all. And to cap it all, his work at the house not done! The roof not finished off, the porch not touched, the hall floor all up. The spandrels! And leaving his friends! No time for even a quick goodbye.

He charged around to try and get dressed. No time for a wash or cleaning his teeth!

"Oh Lord," he cried. "Not today *please*. Help!"

Half way into his clothes he fell against the wall, feeling dizzy.

"Oh it's all too much, all too much – but I must, I must."

He leaned hopelessly on the wall. He glanced to one side; out of the bedroom window. There was Jez in her garden wearing a dressing gown looking at her potato plants. Her husband and a young woman were standing talking with her. They were standing casually, not having to rush away like him. He turned his face desperately to the wall, and bashed it with his fist. He thought at any moment he might have a nervous breakdown. The injustice of it all! A tear rolled down his cheek, and he began to sob. But then the front door knocker was sounding and he heard the driver's voice again.

"Five minutes almost up, sir."

A minute later Seef appeared at the door carrying a jacket and his coat. Clothes and hair all dishevelled and askew. Tear stained face. He felt weak and exhausted. Drained of strength. It was as he began to walk along the garden path he realised he hadn't got any shoes on, and only one sock.

"May I?" he said to the driver pointing down to his feet.

"'Fraid not, sir. We do have to stick to time on this job. It's nice and warm in the car, sir!"

Seef continued staggering up the garden path, not even shutting the front door. The driver followed.

"Sorry about all this sir."

The car door was opened for him. Seef went to get in, but at just the wrong moment, he accidentally dropped his coat and wallet on the pavement and all the contents spilled out. But he was already in the car and the driver had shut the door, not noticing, and when Seef went to try the door it was locked and there was a solid looking glass between him and the driver.

"Oh Lord," he cried, "must *all* be abandoned?"

The car began to move off. Seef more or less doubled over in the back, head down, leaning on his arms. He felt he couldn't have taken one more step and also at that moment he felt he'd been desperately stripped of everything, and was so unhappy with the way things had all been left.

His face was in his hands as he leaned forward on the seat and tears actually began to run down his bare arms. The sleeves and front of the shirt he was wearing were not even fastened. It was fully a minute or two before Seef realised there was actually someone sitting next to him in the back of the car. He looked up. It was Josh!

"Oh Josh," he cried, "what are you doing here?"

"I found out it was your day, and I'm going with you."

"Really! Can it be? Thank you God! Well Josh, you're a sight for sore eyes, you are. A friend just when I needed one! So much has been revealed, Josh! And now it's my flight – so soon - but it's *so* good you're coming with me. I had no idea. And you can't believe what a welcome sight you are! I have been so frustrated, and now I feel bankrupt, with only God Himself to turn to."

"Never mind. Bankrupt and only God to turn to? Best way to be! Sit back and relax. Tell me about it," said Josh.

And so Seef poured out his heart and told everything to Josh as they drove along.

"So practically nothing is even started, never mind finished on the house," concluded Seef. "I haven't been able to set up Staszek, my Polish helper, and now I am being taken to my flight. And the worst thing is that I haven't even had time to go to the police with my evidence."

"Oh, don't worry about *that*," said Josh. "Mi's on his way there right now."

Seef looked at Josh - startled. "He is?"

"Yes, he had his own suspicions you see."

There was a pause.

"Well, that's a great relief anyway," said Seef.

"There were hints and clues that he saw," said Josh. "The book of Jasher said what the animals were doing on the land, and the murderer took up that part to do the deed. The blood was 'crying out' from the ground you remember. I told you I heard a noise!"

"You did. But I have been a fool, thinking of the wrong people all this time."

"Would you ask God to forgive you?"

"I surely will," said Seef looking straight at Josh, tears starting in his eyes again.

"But what about the killer?" asked Josh. "The murderer will be dealt with in the due processes in the courts, but could you forgive from the heart?"

Seef looked again at Josh. He hesitated; but then, as a tear rolled down his cheek, he said, "How can I *not* when I have been forgiven so much myself? I will forgive, as God is my helper."

"Then all is well," said Josh.

"Well! Like Staszek says then!" laughed Seef.

They sat back and drove along in silence for several minutes, looking out of the windows.

"After that day when you told me about all the problems with the new translations," said Seef, "it occurred to me that even if it *was* a satanic plot in the 19th Century to dilute God's word, it didn't succeed – because I know a lot of people who've been converted and helped by the new versions! It's like Satan meant it for evil, but God was able to turn it round for good. The same pattern as for Joseph and his brothers!"

"True," said Josh.

"And then it further occurred to me," Seef continued, "that if the Roman Catholic Church *is*, or turns out to have been some kind of evil plot to drive people away from the Bible and Jesus – as some of our evangelical brethren often say – then *that* didn't succeed either, because a lot of people are also converted and helped through that church! Mi had got fed up with all the liberalism in the Church of England and is actually going to attend the Roman Catholic Church himself. But theological liberalism is growing in there now. And the 'church' is not a good place for inerrant truth to reside - to say the least."

"You could use the same argument about evolution too," remarked Josh. "Some Christians believe in it, yet still progress in faith – yet – I don't think it is God's idea of the best outcome for those kinds of erroneous beliefs – where they do extend into error – to be taken on as they have been."

"I see what you mean. The fact that God gets us through mistakes, doesn't mean that there isn't a better path for us."

"Yes. By the way, when I was telling you the other day about the old Bible compared with the new versions, I didn't really finish off. You might not have picked up that the Textus Sinaiticus was, in my opinion, a 19th Century fraud."

"Fraud? Well I suppose you could call it that."

"I'll tell you the rest of the story if you like – as we have a distance to drive yet. The monks in the Sinai had added a lot of notes to this facsimile. Tischendorf added more, omitted the end of Mark's gospel, and did several things to make it similar to the 'Textus Vaticanus', a text found in the Vatican library that is of very dubious origins, but which certainly isn't ancient."

"Do continue," said Seef. "I need to get my mind off everything that's been swirling around in it."

Josh then began to finish the account about the duplicitous Count Tischendorf, who, ambitious for fortune and fame, said he had 'discovered' the Textus Sinaiticus (but some thought it was it planted for him there by Rome?) when he was out in the Sinai Desert. How at first he thought it was genuine, though he came to realise that it was a fake, but decided he would have to stick with the deceit. Worse for him, he had unfortunately written and criticised one of Simonides' other facsimile works previously, *The Shepherd of Hermes*, which he'd described as a fake. But when he decided to deceive the world with Sinaiticus, he had to retract those comments, or academics would have seen through his own deceit! So he wrote an apology, but in Latin, in an obscure publication that only the academic world would see! So duplicitous!

Simonides, the young but expert calligrapher, who claimed to have written the Sinaiticus document up as well, did these works in a monastery at Mt. Athos in Greece, under his uncle's supervision, who was the chief monk there, around the year 1840. Simonides came out publicly in London and explained that it wasn't meant as a fraud, but intended as a 'replica' – and a gift to the Czar of Russia – in the hope that the Czar would buy them printing press for his uncle's monastery because there was other stuff to publish. But this replica had of course got diverted by other monks to the monastery in Sinai instead after the uncle's death. They seem to have been told at Sinai to amend it. Some forty-three pages of it (two sections) were removed (stolen) by Tischendorf and taken to Germany, where they appeared and were described by viewers of them as 'snow white' in colour. This was the first theft.

Later, the Count, claimed he had 'discovered' the 'oldest and best Bible' out in Sinai, when he went back and stole the rest, but this time, realising that he himself was caught by it being a 'replica', swabbed the pages with lemon juice (when there was a witness) to make the animal skin it was written on – and the ink too – look much older.

Josh had explained that anybody could see the difference between the two stolen parts, as both were now online and everyone could see the change in colour. However, back in the 1860s, once this 'Textus Sinaiticus' was shown to the academic world, it caused them to go back and affirm the authenticity of a similar document, owned and altered about by the Vatican, which had no proper history. This was the Textus Vaticanus, which also had lots of missing passages promoting a liberal type theology and so it was similar, though there were still discrepancies between the two – and with that and the 'Sinaiticus' the so-called 'critical text' was born.

Next Westcott and Hort stepped up to produce the 'definitive text' that they wanted to exist, and thereby they were able to demote the 'Textus Receptus' – and with that, the hated King James Bible. (They had said they wanted to be rid of it.)

"It was a gift to the liberal theologians and modern textual critics; reductionists and deconstructionists who were waiting for something like that," concluded Josh. "It enabled them to have endless nit-picking discussions, about everything! The unlikelihood of miracles; the virtues of unbelief, etc. One example was about whether the account of Jesus rising again and ascending was ever *in* this 'first' gospel of Mark and therefore whether it ever occurred! They wanted very much to have a 'believable' text which really suited all the liberal, so-called 'experts', without any faith, which they could use to relativise Christianity and use to undermine the Authorised Version. And now they had it with these newly 'discovered' tests! And it worked! They could begin to say that perhaps Jesus wasn't raised physically, it not being in the first gospel, and only added to the later ones... Perhaps it was the 'appearance' of a resurrection. And on and on..."

"I've met people who still say that!" added Seef. "Somehow it reminds me of the fake 'early human' skull, the 'Piltdown man', that evolutionists believed in for many years before they found out the jaw was from an ape and the canine teeth had been filed!"

"It's true that people are ready to believe in a deception or lie, if that is what they really want things to be like, and when a bit of even skimpy evidence turns up, they embrace it and it's a 'fact' from then on."

"Why didn't they scientifically test the animal skin and ink using Carbon 14 on the 'Textus Sinaiticus' to find that it was much younger than had been proposed?" asked Seef

"Good question," said Josh. "It's like the police when they looked at the evidence for your father's murder. They missed a lot of clues, even though they were staring them in the face. The fact is the British Museum set up a test but then cancelled it at the last minute. I think they worried that the British Museum would be shown to have been stupid to buy it in the first place and of course it would only be worth peanuts."

"Well, we must forget all that now, I suppose," said Seef. "As well as the Count and the scholars who were involved with deceits, and the churches with all their erroneous and liberal teachings."

"God will be the judge of them. We are coming to a place of answers, not questions; a place of love's reality, not faith; a place of joy, not hope for joy."

They fell quiet.

"Josh?" asked Seef.

"Yes?"

"Notwithstanding what I just said, I've been meaning to ask you – I mean it's been fascinating and all, but why have we spent so long in our times together talking about Bible translation?"

"Again, a good question. When I talk to people about Christianity, I pray to use the right words and subjects. Sometimes I talk about creation or the flood and the lie of evolutionary concepts; sometimes end times, sometimes the work of the Holy Spirit, sometimes the gospel, or the Church, or writers on Christianity, or doctrine and history, or specifics of Bible passages. Sometimes I talk about science and how that argues for God, sometimes suffering, or prayer. In short – I never know, but in your case I felt prompted to talk about Bible translation and the fact we can hold God's actual words in our hands. You had the beginnings of a talk written out about 'What is the Word' on your table one time when I called, and a quick glance showed me your uncertainly. You believed in the Bible being infallible, but you weren't sure why."

"That's right," said Seef. "I couldn't understand how God could be clear and inerrant, when I couldn't

131

understand very well someone like Staszek when he was in the same room! So I thought how can we know for sure? The churches are all run by fallen men and so are not infallible. The Word must be it, I thought, but how? It has to be studied, like I should have done to get the clues for the murder."

"Most Christians are too vague and wishy-washy about the Word," said Josh, "and don't even investigate! I also felt there was a pattern in certain passages there in Genesis, concerning – well – probably lots of layers of things. But there was a sequence or device – a design, strangely enough, to help with solving your poor father's murder, and I had hoped to point you to some help. That's not always what God would do, but in this case I didn't get on very well with *that* aspect of the 'pointing' of it. Then there was the Book of Jasher to help inspire, but not of course part of the canon."

"Sorry I was so dim," said Seef.

"That's okay, but I did wonder with your love of solving mysteries and using clues – your liking of puzzles and card games and the like, whether you might rise to it."

"I should have tried shouldn't I!" said Seef. They looked out of the car window at the countryside flashing past.

"We've still got a little way to go to the airport; would you like another challenge to think about?" asked Josh. "Well, it's a teaser actually."

"I probably *do* need something else too to distract my thoughts from my own concerns. What is it?"

"Could you compose a short written genealogy?"

"Yes. Easily. I studied some of our family history at one time."

"Alright. But there are some rules before you take the challenge on."

"Ok."

"The first is that you have to understand the importance of the number seven," said Josh.

"Ah yes. I know about that. A very Biblical number. The number for Jesus Christ! It's funny how God loves certain numbers. I think the number seven is one of His favourites. I suppose this numerology business has been hijacked since (I guess) ancient times by an interest in the occult, and paranormal delvers and the like."

"That's true. But numbers *began* with God and creation," said Josh, "not the devil! It's the same with the

133

signs in the stars and constellations, set there by God to be decoded by people on Earth."

"You told me it is the glory of God to conceal a matter and the glory of kings to search it out," cried Seef. "Proverbs 25:2!"

"Exactly," said Josh. "That's how the three kings were able to wisely unearth the secret of the Messiah's birth – looking for signs in the heavens. And we've forgotten these God-given arts. And, as you know, for every good thing, there's always a corruption, and the devil *has* corrupted that art by bringing in *astrology*, an occult practice. The difference is that astrologers search, as they think, for people's personal destinies – that's all hogwash. Godly 'kings' and wise enquirers look for the purpose God has for his people and in the world, and refer back to the Bible. That's how we knew about the Revelation 12 sign in the heavens recently. You know when Jupiter (the King Planet) was in the 'womb' of Virgo for exactly nine months, at exactly the same time as the moon was under her feet and she was 'clothed' with the sun and had, upon her head a crown of twelve stars! (These were the planets and stars visible to the naked eye.) We await the signs in the rest of the passage!

Anyway, also, as you probably know, the whole gospel story, known from creation and Adam's time, is right there in the twelve (another Bible number!) constellations of the stars – but as we've said, again hijacked by the *astrologers* and used by the occult arts like some aspects of numerology has been... How did I get onto this?"

"You were about to give me a challenge and you said I had to remember the importance of the number seven!"

"Oh yes. Sorry! And you have to compile a genealogy statement. Are you ready?"

"Yes."

"The first thing is that your little written piece about your genealogy must consist of a total number of words that is divisible by 7."

"I think I could manage that very easily."

"Next, you have to count up the number of letters in all your words and they must also add up to be divisible by 7."

"Ah, now that's trickier, but I think I could just about manage that if you give me a little time."

"There's more. And the next thing is that all the vowels, and all the consonants must add up to be divisible by 7."

"Give me a break! I can't manage that – it's probably impossible!"

"No – it's definitely possible, and I'm not finished. The total number of words that begin with a vowel must also be divisible by seven, and the words that begin with a consonant must also be divisible by seven. Those that occur in more than one form must divide by seven, and those that only occur in *one* form, also divide by seven."

"Ridiculous!"

"Wait. Also the number of nouns must divide by seven, there must only be seven non-nouns. Seven names, seven generations – are you still *in*?"

"No! Crazy! – and totally, totally impossible by the way!"

"You probably haven't guessed where I'm going, but this is the genealogy of Jesus Christ as set out in Matthew 1, 1-11. By the way, of course, it's in the Textus Receptus; it's all in Greek – which is a very rigid and precise language. The passage right there in Matthew meets *all* these rules! By the way it doesn't work in the 'corrupted' Egyptian Greek manuscripts, only in the Textus Receptus. "

"Really? Does it? All of those rules? Now that is astounding!"

"I've given you *nine* rules so far," said Josh, "and statistically the chances of achieving that – are 40 million to one."

"Impossible in other words humanly speaking."

"I'm telling you, to get over the truth that I want to emphasise – this book, God's word, and the passages in it are *beyond* human capabilities; and this kind of structure in the scriptural text has been *designed* by someone outside our space and time. These features are *not* simulatable – even with a computer. And the puzzle I set you gets worse and worse by the way. Greek letters have numerical values, and totalling up of the numbers shows up dozens more things divisible by seven. So there are not 9 rules but actually - 34 in total! And there was a Russian, a Dr Ivan Panin, who died in 1855, who claims he found as many as 75 rules."

"No wonder the Russians always do well at chess," laughed Seef.

"Dr Panin also discovered Christ for himself – a yet greater miracle!" said Josh.

"I say 'Amen' to that, and 'praise the Lord'. To walk with Him every day until we're called home is the supernatural Christian life."

"My point is, in all these talks and in going through all these kinds of details in the Bible with you, that we confirm we have a staggering and supernatural design in the Scriptures. The whole New Testament and indeed the Old too, has these patterns of seven! For example, if you look at the vocabulary that is unique to the whole gospel of Matthew and not found in the other gospels, the number of new words there can also be divided by seven. You could say, well that was easy, all Matthew had to do was write his gospel last and make sure all the new words divided by seven – except – that when you go back to Mark, *that* has the same property, *and* Luke, *and* John, *and* even the writings of James, Peter and Paul. So they are all unique. They can't all have been written last!"

"There are many, I suppose, who would say, 'So what?'. The main thing is not that, but obeying Jesus."

"It *is* important for us to be obedient. But I believe Scripture itself teaches us that obedience and our good works emanate from faith, not our human endeavours. And when you ask yourself what is faith, and what do you believe in, you come back to how much you trust the Bible, and if so, which version? The Textus Receptus meets all these criteria but not the others. So it seems that it is important to be absolutely sure that you know – beyond any doubt whatsoever – that you can trust the word. And, to that end, I would argue with those who say something like, 'You can never prove the Bible, so all things must be taken on faith', I would say, 'you *can* prove the Bible, and that makes faith – and works – even stronger'. And so I tried to convince you in our talks that we, with the Bible – where I promoted the King James – are handling a supernatural integrated communication system."

"Which, as you said Josh, Scripture is itself a miracle outside our time and space references. Oh, this looks like some kind of an airfield.

"Yes, this is the place, but did you find our Bible chats helpful?" asked Josh.

"I did. Yes. I think I only half believed about the Textus Receptus before. Your words were certainly scratching where it itched as far as I was concerned."

"Good. I always think Christian people should constantly pray in order to know what's best to say in situations. I think it's important about the Bible – to

139

know. This is an area, like so many areas, where liberals have made belief so difficult. I didn't mention it just now but sometimes I tell stories, even fairy stories! Also parables and use symbolic illustrations. You see, sometimes with people, you have to clear the ground, so that they, for a moment might believe the supernatural and miracles are really possible. And sometimes a story – or a testimony – does it best. You know the Lord Jesus told parables!   But we *have* to believe in the supernatural, like the resurrection. And if we haven't got the right habit of mind, we won't."

"True," Seef said. "I always think that being surrounded by the natural and the secular world is a continuous obstacle to belief."

"Yes, indeed. Ah! We're close. We *are* now coming up to the airport gate. Our flight is from the far side so we don't need all the formalities."

They drove around the outside of the runway areas and pulled into an area well away from the buildings. They got out of the car.

"What is all this water here Josh?" said Seef, realising that there was a lake or river between them and the waiting plane.

"Oh yes. They have flooding in this place and they

don't seem to be able to stop it. Every time I've come this way it has occurred. It's very, very rare the flood isn't here."

"But I won't make it through *that* – it looks cold and deep," said Seef. "I'm not feeling particularly strong at the moment. I don't even have any shoes."

"That's why I'm here," said Josh. "I'll be next to you if you slip."

"It doesn't look as if there's any other way," said Seef, looking across towards the distant plane and all around.

"No, there isn't."

"Well let's press on then."

They began to wade in. It struck cold, but then Seef got a little used to it. At first he wished he'd brought his waders, never mind shoes, but they would have been no good. The water was much deeper than waders could cope with. At the deepest point Seef slipped and almost gave up, but he reached out and Josh took his hand. Then soon they found the water getting shallower.

"There are some warm dry things in the plane," said Josh.

There was a cool wind so Seef was glad to be climbing the steps of the aircraft. The captain was there and looked briefly into his eyes.

"Welcome aboard," he said.

He was soon into the dry things provided inside and the stewardess brought some hot tea. They were taxiing the aircraft.

"Where are the other passengers?" asked Seef.

"There's only us," laughed Josh. "Why don't you relax and have a nap? It's quite a long flight."

Seef looked out of the window and leaned back. He *did* feel tired. It had been a late night and an early morning and his dip in the water had taken it out of him. He was asleep in minutes.

Chapter Eleven

The Gift

Seef had some pleasant dreams. He dreamed he was back with his father and mother at home. Except it wasn't their old home. They were having a wonderful reunion of the family and celebrating and talking about old times. It was so nice. Wherever it was they were, it was *super* nice; a kind of lovely mansion with glorious gardens. He wanted to get back to the dream as he became aware he was waking up, but he couldn't open his eyes. From the next seat, Josh was looking at him, smiling.

"How are you feeling?"

"Much better thanks – in fact I feel totally reinvigorated." He had been once in a hyperbaric oxygen chamber and that felt refreshing, but now he felt a thousand times better than that had made him feel. He told Josh, who laughed.

"The hyperbaric chamber was more like the atmosphere of the early earth when our ancestors lived so long! Ah! It's good you feel well. It's not too long now before we land."

"But somehow, Josh, it felt like I slept for a hundred years!"

"Yes, people say that. Oh right, the seatbelt warning light has just come on. We need to 'belt up'." The hostess came and checked and they went through the usual slow descent process. If anything it seemed even longer than usual.

Finally through the aircraft window he began to see a green and tree-filled land. There were sparkling blue lakes and here and there large houses visible. Further off were distant hills and snow capped mountains. Then with hardly a bump the plane landed and taxied once again out to what seemed like the edge of an airfield next to fields where the grass gently waved. Finally the seatbelt lights switched off. They walked to the exit door of the plane and out into the sunshine. The air certainly felt fresh and invigorating.

"Welcome to Beulah, Seef! No luggage to bring makes it so easy," cried Josh cheerfully. They stood looking at the meadows and fields before them. There were grassy areas mainly, with patches of wild flowers dotted about.

Seef breathed in the air. It felt as if a draft of happiness and new life came in with the air. Nice fragrances and scents on the hint of a breeze! No tiredness today. Seef thought he'd never felt better. He felt as he had many years before as a child, on the eve of an exciting holiday.

Down the aircraft steps they went. At the bottom of the steps there was a waiting transport bus. The white-clad driver looked as if he was delighted to see them. All smiles. They stepped on board. It was the kind of luxury coach that had fewer seats. Between the seats were racks full of fresh fruit and exotic flowers, but Seef felt he wouldn't try the fruit just then.

They took their places and drove away from the airport area into the clean boulevard type streets that lay beyond the fields. Seef thought it looked a very pleasant place; full of majestic trees and flowering shrubs. Some leaves were red or gold. After a mile or two the bus turned up a side turning into a small road that was winding upwards into the hills. In between the leaves there were the occasional large houses appearing. In one place Josh briefly saw a cluster of houses together around a village green. After a few minutes the bus came to the end of the road and made a circle as if to turn.

"We can walk from here," said Josh, smiling.

There was a gravelly path meandering through the

trees which they walked together. Again, flowers either side of the little track. After a few minutes a huge mansion became visible off to one side.

"Wow," said Seef. "Now that's what I call opulence!"

"Yes and it hasn't been occupied too long either."

There was something like a barbecue or garden party going on out on one of the terraces. Some of the people there waved at Josh and Seef in a friendly manner, and they waved back.

"Now in England that would be a billionaire's house," said Seef.

"The owner has inherited great wealth since coming here," said Josh and paused. "He was very poor before, that was for sure. In fact we both know him. It's Dick Grub's residence, and he's having a small party!"

"Dick Grub! No! Are you joking?"

"No I'm not. He loves parties, and wining and dining with guests and having friends around. He loves it in there!"

"I expect he does!" Seef cried, remembering Dick's old life.

"Well, although it's set in the countryside here, which he loves," explained Josh, "he really likes his new home with its gold chandeliers and taps and all the special details. He found he also loves giving parties and having guests too. Nobody is rude to him here! Also he likes showing people around the extensive grounds. They go on for miles and there's lots of wildlife in them as well. He always did love God and all His creatures, you know. And you have to smile at him now getting whatever he fancies from the larder and giving it to his guests. I can get you an invite - if you like?"

"Can you? Really? I would love that. I could apologise to him in person for being stupid enough to suspect him."

"Not right now though," said Josh. "I want to show you *your* accommodation."

They walked on further, past a field of sheep and lambs. One pair looked exactly like Weelike and her own lamb.

"I'm sure I know those two!" cried Seef. He went over and they seemed to recognise him, nuzzling their noses in his hand. "Just like home around here!" cried Seef.

"Yes! We're getting near your place. You've guessed it!" laughed Josh.

They took another path through the trees. There

were a few of Seef's favourite flowers alongside the path. Off to one side there were views of the distant hills and mountains.

"This reminds me of some of the walks I had years ago!" said Seef.

"Yes," said Josh, "but get ready now – I've been waiting for this moment – I actually couldn't wait to see your face when you see what's ahead!"

They turned a corner and a view opened up of a beautiful large house on rising ground. There was a sparkling blue lake to one side with a jetty, a boat house, and a boat tied up.

"It's Amen House!" cried Seef, staring at it. "No it's not – it's larger - and it's what I imagined Amen House *could* have looked a bit like if I'd had *all* the work done. But it's better than Amen House could have been. Why that front elevation is *exactly* as I was planning to do it - but better! Wow! And look at the spandrels over the porch!"

"I thought you'd like it," said Josh, grinning. "Will this be all right for you then? But no – don't say yes until you've had a chance to look around."

Josh then took him on a tour over the whole place. Inside it *was* a bit like Seef's home, Amen House, back in England, but every feature about it was superior. After a while they stopped in the room that Seef had imagined would be a library once he had done all the work. But it was way larger than in the Amen House back in Kings Sternton. This particular room was much better fitted out than he'd imagined his would be *and* considerably higher. It was now the kind of library he might have dreamed about.

"Well?" said Josh. He looked at Seef.

But Seef was in tears.

"Is this for me to use?" he asked.

"Of course."

"This is so much more than I deserve," Seef said. "How can I ever pay you for such a gift?"

"You can't!" said Josh. "Though there is another thing I'd like you to do, but I won't explain it just yet. Meantime I'd like to show you something else."

Josh led Seef outside and along the front of the house where there was a view into the middle distance. Several large houses could be seen. One Chinese style house, with its multiple layers of roof, stood out.

"You see the property with the Cantonese style elevations over there?"

"Oh yes, that looks rather stunning."

"That's for Mi."

"Really? Is he coming to Beulah too?"

"He is, in the next few weeks or so. Perhaps you'll be able to meet him and give him a welcome?"

"Certainly!"

"Thank you. Meantime I urge you to relax and enjoy yourself for a while. There's some snorkelling equipment in the boat house over there for when you want a swim in the lake, and plenty of stuff you'll find interesting to read in the library. There's a cosy fire in that room for the evenings, as you might have seen. But anyway, I have to leave you for now. For food and everything else there's an older lady coming this evening who particularly wanted to welcome you too; Mrs Welch."

"Mrs Welch! I met the old dear! She's here too? This is all so surprising. What a wondrous place! I suppose the arrangements and times, or something, must be different here from England. Anyway, Josh, thank you so much for all of this beautiful accommodation. It makes me feel unworthy – yet so grateful at the same time. Are there any others here I will know?" asked Seef with a laugh.

"Well there's a *lot* more people to meet you over 'time', but don't rush it; and you'll get used to not bothering about time here, as well – you'll be surprised how soon you'll forget it altogether – and also there are many other places to see here yet – but again for the moment you just need to settle in, relax, and find your feet. By the way there are plenty of clothes in the wardrobe upstairs. Have a look! There's even a drawing board if you fancy a bit of architecture. I need a garden shed designed for your grounds!"

"Okay," said Seef, smiling.

Then Josh walked away. As he did, he shouted out over his shoulder.

"Don't forget to try the boat out! There's a lot of interesting dive sites and coves further afield, and connecting lakes to get there - and the fish and underwater life out there are stunning! Have fun!"

Seef stood there and waved in a kind of daze with a permanent smile on his face. This was going to be the most amazing time!

Chapter Twelve

Rewards

Seef went back into the house with a new spring in his step. He went upstairs and looked in the wardrobes of the lavish bedroom. All the casual clothes and suits and shirts were his size and the kind he liked to wear, as well as some other much grander outfits – and even great robes and coronets, and a crown hanging up and placed there - all of which greatly astonished him. He wondered why the things might be there, but he had a feeling of awe about what they might be for, which made him feel a sort of suppressed excitement.

Then he went down into the library. It was a tall room with books to the ceiling and little mobile ladders and landings to reach the book shelves. He randomly took one great leather bound work down, then another, and he gradually became more and more surprised, the more he looked into the volumes; there seemed to be *all* of the books he had treasured back in England – and ever wanted - and many more ancient and interesting ones he had never come across. Lots of new ones were there as well. It seemed as if someone had gone to a lot of trouble to gather them all - just to suit him. All the early fathers and doctors of the faith were there and many of the early philosophers too. He noticed a lovely edition of Plato and an impressive looking King James Bible. There was even a puzzle book or two.

He was just browsing through an ancient edition of Josephus (he found it didn't have the mistake of many editions that had made Herod's death date wrong, and consequently people had miscalculated Christ's birth date) – when he heard a voice at the front door.

"'Ello Seef ducks! 'Ow is you? Everything all right for ya?"

"Mrs Welch! – do come in!" said Seef running into the hall. He felt so pleased to see her that he even gave her a hug.

"Nice to see you too luv! Now I must confess – I found out since I come to this 'ere country, that I've bin a bit of a gossip – but they's 'elping me, so I's changin' now, so anyways I asked 'em – the powers that be – if I could come up 'ere an' 'elp you get settled in like, 'fore I moves on. They said yes and so I got in some of ya favourite bits and pieces in the pantry. A nice bit o' bacon an' eggs an' a decent sized lamb joint for in a day or two if ya want a guest for dinner."

"Oh! You're so good Mrs Welch! I haven't even looked in the pantry. But where are you 'moving on' to?"

"Well luv, once ya finds yer feet around 'ere like, there are trips and visits "igher up' in the 'mountain country' towards the centre of this 'ere country. They sez it's amazing. I 'spec they'll tell you about it too when they is ready. They say you get to meet the king."

"Well now you've got me curious – I'm very happy to have come – but that's an insufficient word – at the moment I love just being around here!"

"Just so, Seef luv. Now then, I know as 'ow you like a nice breakfast – but it's got to more like lunch time now! And then we brought zum of that nice English draft beer for ya – the IPA – same ale as they 'ad in the pub near Kings Sternton. But they sez it's much better 'ere. The barrels in the basement will be kept nice and cool."

"Really? I didn't know there was a basement! Well, a pint of that would be really nice just now (as it's lunch time) and then – well – could I have a full English breakfast *now* please?" Seef realised that he hadn't had breakfast before he left or eaten anything at all for many hours.

"Course ya can luv," she said cheerfully. "All day

breakfast! Eggs, bacon, beans, toms and fried spuds coming up! I got in some other stuff for a nice curry tonight as well – if that's okay with ya, Seef dear?"

"Mrs Welch – you're a saint!"

"That's what they keep callin' me round 'ere!" she said, laughing. "I'm only jus' a gettin' used to it! I'll give ya a shout when breakfast is ready, ducks!"

And so it went on like that for Seef and Mrs Welch for quite a few days. Sometimes Seef sat in the garden. If anything, he thought, that was the only place needing a bit of attention. In the evenings he read voraciously and in the day went exploring in the boat and snorkelling too. Water sports had always been his hobby but he never seemed to have the energy or the time back in England. Here in Beulah he had both. He even started on the shed design mentioned by Josh.

One day Mrs Welch said to him that she had heard Mr. Mi had moved in. "Or so they sez in the village, luv."

"Really! I'll walk over and see if I can see him straight away," cried Seef. He took the little path going that way and on arrival, found he had indeed moved in, and very happy he was too with the arrangements. Seef formerly welcomed him. It was so good for him to see

Mi again and for them both to catch up. They talked about all the news as well as the new-found thrills of the lovely place they had come to. Mi showed him all around his new house.

"Was big surprise for me, Mr. Seef," he said, laughing. "And all rooms are like my home as child in China – which I always loved."

Seef noticed in the furnishings and décor, that as well as the Cantonese style, there were one or two things reminiscent of Catholic and Orthodox influences too – the sort of thing he imagined Mi might like – and Mi confirmed it by grinning away at it all.

They were chatting away when suddenly there was a call at the door – and Josh surprisingly appeared. He was carrying a tray of Chinese sweetmeats as a welcome present for Mi.

"Oh Mr. Josh – sweetmeats! Like my Chinese home – this completes my happiness," Mi cried. He almost looked as if he would burst into tears.

Seef greeted Josh too. He hadn't seen him again since their arrival. And Seef had an even greater respect for him now since he'd seen all the things he'd arranged in Beulah, but he had a few questions as well.

"Before you ask," said Josh, "I wanted to tell you

that you're both welcome to Dick's big barbecue banquet tomorrow. Can you come?"

"Yes please!" they both said, laughing.

"'What larx' we're having!" cried Seef.

"Now what about your questions, Seef?" Josh began to lead him to a seat outside the house, while Mi said he would see about lunch.

"I love to cook here!" called out Mi as he went to his kitchen. "I do special for you today!"

"Talking about Dick Grub just then reminds me of one of the questions, Josh," said Seef. He stopped, uncertain how to say it. "We see some of our friends here, especially Christians, but I was just wondering about some of the *other* people who weren't, well, say for example, Big Jim?"

"I'll tell you in a moment about 'Big Bad' Jim. But first I wanted to mention about Rosemary."

"Rosemary? The woman he lived with?"

"Yes. You might be interested to know *she* came here – to one of Dick's parties – just the other night. She always looked to the Lord *at heart*, you know. So now she's undergoing a process of healing really; and she's gradually coming round. The air here is good for her here. I reckon she'll soon forget the rotten years she spent. The other thing to explain, Seef, concerns another location.   It is that which I'm about to show you, and it is a picture of a place that is a long, long way from here. In fact it's impossible to get there from here, and we're unable to change things there in any way."

"Picture? Far away? What d'you mean?"

"Well, you were asking about Big Jim?"

"Oh yes."

"Because I had been wondering if you'd ask something like that. Let me see." He drew what looked like an electronic tablet out of his jacket pocket. "This one has the 'app' I think." He moved his finger. "Ah yes. This is a live feed to where Big Jim is now – but I warn you it's not a pretty sight."

Seef wondered what it could possibly be he was about to see regarding Big Bad Jim – and to see it on Josh's tablet too. Still – technology now! – and no reason why it shouldn't be even *better* here than back in England! He took the tablet from him and looked. It was the place where Big Jim was residing certainly, for there he was, as plain as day. But his surroundings were truly terrible, as shockingly torturous as they could be.   What a place! It couldn't have looked worse for Big Bad Jim. After a minute he handed the tablet back. He was silent for a moment and in thought.

"You're right," he said. "I don't think I want to see something like that ever again. And you say there's nothing can be done for him?"

"No. All that could be done *was* done, years ago. He turned God down in his heart, time after time. And it's best not to think about it now – cast it from your mind. You will find you soon forget it - even after a few minutes – like when you wake up after a dream. I've been trying to warn his son, 'Monkey Boy', about not following his dad so that he goes to that place, but it's not working. It seems to be so hard to get through to people these days. Back in Kings Sternton, Monkey Boy seems to have been captured by the evil one, and has got in hand some proposed changes in the village – and they're certainly not good ones. One of them is that he is trying to change the parish church into some kind of combination of night club and dressing up bar. The bishop – who is a theological liberal – had bizarrely suggested a 'Gender Experimentation Clinic and Parlour' where people could dress up in the opposite sex's clothes and see how they feel; and then they could have (secular) counselling about their sexuality. So Monkey Boy's doing a version of it with booze and dancing. The church! Can you believe it? But enough of them and all that.

Now, about someone else you know. Jez. She's experienced a 'severe mercy'. I say severe in the best way for her. Jezzy, as she now calls herself, suffered pretty hard in the prison. But she's fully repented and been wonderfully changed – and for the best."

"Goodness me Josh – good for her - but so much is changing – and in such short order too!" cried Seef.

"It might seem short to you! Remember times are different here! But now," said Josh, "I come to the favour I wanted to ask you. Shall we walk or sit in the garden while Mi enjoys finishing his cooking? We'll be back for when it's ready."

"Yes, why not?" Mi came out from the kitchen at that moment and called out that food would be a good half hour or so.

"Do look at my garden, Mr. Seef," he shouted. "It is best place of all. It exactly same as Chinese garden on my willow pattern plate at King Sternton! You will be amazed, I think."

They wandered into Mi's garden. A magical place indeed! All the lovely exotic plants and shrubs! The scents! The little painted bridges! The trickling water features! The little Chinese summer house facing it all! That's where Josh and Seef went and sat, overlooking a real live willow-pattern scene – minus the actors in the willow pattern plot, of course!

"First, I want to show you this," said Josh.

Josh showed Seef the media report of his father's murder:

Murder in Kings Sternton

The murder of Sebastian Able in the village last summer has at last been solved. The victim's neighbour, Mrs Jezebel Cain, has been convicted of the crime.

It appears that Mr Able had had a dispute with Mrs Cain concerning an agreed right of way over part of Cain's land. The right of way that Mr Able had been using to his field cut across the corner of the defendant's land.

It was explained in court that Mr Able's animals, which were believed to be two sheep, had been eating some of Mrs Cain's crops during their short crossing of their land, and a row had then broken out between them.

Apparently the Cains had parked a plough across the entrance to the right of way to deter access, but Mr Able had ignored this. Mrs Cain pleaded guilty to poisoning the sheep, which had then dropped dead on Mr Able's lawn, and then she had removed one of the iron bars from the aforesaid plough and used it to strike Mr Able down in the hallway of his home.

In her defence, Mrs Cain said she had been guilty of an "act of madness" and was desperately sorry. The court noted that she had showed great contrition after her arrest and this fact was taken into account in her sentence.

The police commended Mr Mi Nayaboor, Mr Able's other neighbour, a Chinese gentleman, who had first alerted them to the crime and later gave them the iron bar, which was the piece of evidence that helped clinch the verdict. But the police were criticised by the court for not making further enquiries about Cain. The police inspector said in their defence that they had been busy on "other lines of enquiry".

Seef handed back the report to Josh. "That last part was partly my fault!" he said, and then he told Josh he decided he would try and put it all behind him.

"You *will* be able to here," said Josh.

"And yes, my favour is all about Jezzy," said Josh after they had both sat for a further while soaking in the scene. "She was one of those who started well but then went terribly wrong. I will tell you her story. As a little girl she was 'good and obedient' and loved growing flowers and fruit in her parents' garden. She went to Sunday school and at a very young age she gave her heart to Jesus. From that point Jesus looked after her as far as she would let him – but by the time she got to university she got in with a bad crowd and went off the tracks. It came with an addiction that you saw hints of in her house.

"God only helps us while we let Him, you know! She actually continued going to church but she was very nominal and her heart was far, far away. People just don't seem to get it that God looks on the heart. Yielding up to the 'King of Hearts' will set them right. But people think God's not looking there in the inside of them!"

"She married (poor George!) and got busy with 'third wave' feminism and sexual laxity in the church type issues and also her heart kept straying to that same temptation she had indulged in from university days. It made her become quite aggressive with those who stood up to her. She got a bit more masculine and butch and by the time she moved to Kings Sternton to grow potatoes, the King of Heaven, whom she'd half forgotten about, was getting ready to be stern with her. (She didn't oversee the pun in it – 'King's Stern town!') But, as often happens, things were going to get much worse before they got better."

A highly coloured humming bird came up to Josh and Seef, hovered in front as if listening, then quickly darted away.

"So tame here! Glory to God!" exclaimed Seef.

"Mixed with Jezzy's other issue was pride, which showed itself in the way she thought of her potatoes, but also in her feminist LGBT type work for the diocese. But her problems all culminated with a particular Harvest Festival at the church which triggered off a disastrous sequence of events."

"Harvest Festival! Really?" said Seef.

"She presented her harvest offering at the church, a sack of potatoes. It was going to be given to the poor. But it wasn't the best of the crop; because she had kept that back for herself. (She said to herself it was only going to the poor and it didn't matter.) It was your father, Seef, who had to sort the harvest food out for the poor, including her potatoes."

"My dad?"

"Yes, and when he opened up the sack he found quite a few rotten spuds, so he quietly tried to get rid of the worst. But she came to the church that particular day at that very hour and found him doing the sorting – then there was a row.

"After that she went around telling people that the potatoes were all fine but *he* had kept all the best ones for *himself*, and she told them that your father hadn't put anything in the harvest collection himself. This wasn't true - he'd supplied the meat for the Irish stew supper - but she said it anyway, and then added, 'All he did for the harvest was say a silly prayer.' (This was because your father stood up in church at the harvest and said a prayer saying, 'Thank you for harvest but we thank you even more for Jesus.') Jez sneered and tried to belittle him. Anyway, after that she came to entirely hate him (sin was 'crouching at the door' and hatred took possession of her).

"She next tried to close up the right of way in the garden that the sheep and the lamb were using for access to the field. She planted on it. But your father was firm, saying that he was entitled to use it. So that was another row. It made her so furious that she rushed back into her house and – in her anger – she found some rat poison and fed it to Weelike. It killed the sheep but didn't affect the lamb because it was only taking her milk at that time; only just starting to graze. The lamb ran away when she tried to grab it.

"Your father was so upset when he saw what had happened – because he put two and two together – that he said he would have to report it to the police. Then she became a real wild cat! She went and found, on top of her plough, one of the linking iron bars that was loose and went round to Amen House intending to beat him up a bit. She hadn't intended to kill him, but one of the blows she dealt in her anger struck a blood vessel in his neck and he fell down bleeding profusely on the hall floor – to rise no more – in that world, anyway."

"Poor dad!"

"She pulled up the carpet in the hall a bit, saw the boards were rotten, and she pushed the murder weapon through a gap. Then she fled. Your poor father's blood soaked the carpet and even dripped down through the boards to the ground beneath.

"In spiritual terms sin was crouching at her door, you see, and she couldn't master it. It had mastered her. After you left the village to come here Mi got suspicious, as I told you, and came round to Amen House. The door was open and he saw the plough part on the hall floor and put two and two together. He showed the police the bar with the blood on it that you had dug up from below the floorboards. They arrested Jez and checked and found her prints and DNA all over it, as well as your dad's blood. So she was locked up, awaiting trial.

"After that Jez was so sorry and humbly asked the

166

Lord to help her make amends. She repented before God of her crime. There she sat in her cell with tears running down her face. Her heart, you see, was not a bad heart at root – it's just that she was weak in spite of her outward bravado. Anyway she confessed her guilt to the police and because of her contrition was given a partially suspended sentence – but in a tough jail. So it was in prison she had a wretched time. But, as I said, she came through, and as she finally broke down further and fully repented before the Lord for *all* her wrongs over the years as well as her sexually wrong lifestyle, she was realising, as she read her Bible, especially in Romans I, how offensive it all was to God. She saw for the first time how her life had gradually gone downhill from when she was a young girl growing flowers and fruit in her parents' garden. The Lord graciously granted her full repentance. I'll explain.

"She came across C S Lewis's essays about democracy and equality. She initially thought that she could prove him wrong, but she saw that 'equality' might actually be only a *'medicine'* if we lived in a *fallen* world! She realised she had based her whole worldview on what the P C 'woke' culture had told her, which was not only worldly but fed her own self-importance. For the first time, she saw that she based everything on the subjective feelings that she had been told to follow, and there was no objectivity, nor an ounce of humility in it.

"She also read *The Poison of Subjectivism* by C S Lewis and realised that the Bible said nothing about equality and feminism, but a great deal about humility and repentance. Feminine equality of opportunity was a good thing, however, but equality of *outcome* contradicted that! She was sorry she had listened so much to the spirit of worldliness.

"She had come to see how her ardent and extreme political views had taken her away from God. She saw how first-wave feminism was good, but how the rest was an idea from the 'Zeitgeist' of the world, and not Biblical at all. She saw that she had been using feminism and sexual perversion as a weapon of hate, not love. Before, she even used to give talks on 'Toxic Masculinity' and the poison of 'Patriarchy' and the 'Rape Culture'! But she saw that she had only been denying the divine *ultimate* Patriarchy and Masculinity found in the love of God the Father! Once she accepted Him again, she found the way was clear to see men in the correct way. She realised that what the world needed was not aggressive feminism, but strong, noble and *responsible* masculinity, and that males would be more like this with good and godly women encouraging them, and if the men too followed God the Father. She also realised that she had not been a good wife to George. And she saw that her work had been destroying the church from within. She saw much else. And when she discovered the great mercy and grace of God, in addition to His severity to deal with sin, she was ready, truly ready, to be a true woman of God.

"Anyway, thankfully, when she had served her time," continued Josh, "there was an opportunity for her to come here. She was driven to the airport leaving behind her husband and Lily, who was lodging in another house in King's Sternton (Lily is still living in the village and has just joined the Bible class. I have my hopes!).

"But God often has severe mercy, as I've said. There was a very bad accident on the way to the airport and the car went up in flames. She only *just* managed to get out - but was badly shaken and burned, and of course all her clothes were scorched and torn. So the other day when she arrived here she was literally stinking of smoke with hardly a stitch on to keep her decent. She herself was saved, you see, but only as from the flames of a fire.

"She begged and pleaded for a certain role to do here – and now I come to my point. She was so anxious to beg your forgiveness – I told her that she already had that – but she wanted to tell you personally and serve you in some humble capacity and find a way in which to do something for you. It's been decreed that she *could* have a role, if it's all right with you. She can grow flowers and fruit and beautify your garden, and live in your new 'shed', but she needs your permission as well to do so." Josh paused. "What do you say?"

Josh looked at Seef. Seef looked up, light and tears dancing in his eyes.

"I say yes," he said.

"Good, you have chosen right! How I love a reconciliation! Forgiveness is so powerful. It's actually a supernatural grace," said Josh. "And we might note in passing that there is a little parable applicable here of how Christians can fall out over the wrong things. The illustration I'm thinking of might also appeal to you with your sense of history."

"How? What?"

"Well you might have noticed that Protestants can

be quite happy if people talk about large rewards in heaven – or lesser rewards – that is, that when people have gold, silver or precious stones to 'bring' they are rewarded more, but if they have only wood, hay or stubble they are not rewarded so much – but they are all still saved of course! The in-between ones, they may qualify for in-between rewards. In the parable that Jesus tells of the wise steward (Luke 12), there are three categories; the *bad* servant - will die (v.46) and go to the unbelievers' place - hell; the servant who should have known *better* but did nothing - will be beaten with 'many stripes', while the servant who knew *not* and did not commit things worthy of a thrashing - will be beaten with only a few stripes (v.47/8). Different rewards, different punishments, you see? So to bring it to what you're beginning to see here, the reward may be to live in a mansion or perhaps – if less rewarded – to *serve* in a mansion, or even, if you will, have to bed down in a shed in the garden of someone's mansion! (All the same people may progress to something better!) What's happening here with Mrs Welch and Jezzy could be seen as an indistinct picture of all that."

"Oh! Yes, I see that now. Yes, that makes sense."

"So, this is a view most evangelicals might accept.

And on the other hand, when the Catholics talk of, say purgatory, or punishments or beatings if you like, where people have to go through things in order to get to their final reward - all these categories can still apply. They are still all saved on both of their views you see! But with both interpretations there are rewards – or not – and so the Catholics and Protestants end up saying more or less the same thing – both 'right' - but you could say they're merely using different words.

Josh paused. "And I expect you can see how some principle like that might possibly have applied in European history. Back in the Reformation, both Catholics and Protestants who were devout - not all were - had the same *common* ground in Christ. In Hindsight it was tragic really. The devout *both* believed in justification by faith for example, before and after the Reformation. They put words and sometimes misleading statements in each other's mouths! The irony was that in some cases devout Catholics did their bits of so-called work, trusting totally in Christ for salvation, while in other cases some of the dodgier Protestants were actually *working* for their rewards and had even strayed away from a 100% trust in justification by faith to do so. It was a tragic situation really.

"And it was miserable to see, when all that controversy was playing out about indulgences, relics and pardons, etcetera, that their *hearts* were closed to each other when they were so *close*. They gloried over what they *said* the other side believed, even if it wasn't always true. Tragic that deep inside, many a heart on both sides was actually united - and united to Christ - they were so close; the gap was so narrow!

"To say a Protestant like Tyndale had a doctrine of faith that dispensed with works is a gross misunderstanding. Works are not a saving thing, but an inseparable result or fruit that goes with faith. When Tyndale talked of 'faith', his Catholic opponents meant the same thing but they called it 'charity'. Both sides often meant the same thing you see, but they were using different words – and they were ready to hate, be cruel, and even kill each other for the difference! And then to compound it and make it all worse, both sides had taken to saying things their opponents didn't even really *believe* at all, and they gleefully triumphed over them for positions they didn't actually hold! As you know, after that, they just went on and killed each other. Christians who claimed they both loved Jesus. Both sides did it!

"The truth is we only have faith, charity (agape love) – and forgiveness – by God's grace. And his grace is found in Jesus Christ. I expect you can see now why I said forgiveness is a divine grace. People tend to forget that the Lord's Prayer says, 'Forgive us our trespasses *as we* forgive those who trespass against us.'"

"Yes – but what a horrible mess we weave and have woven for ourselves!" cried Seef.

"The Lord always looks at the inside of us, not the outside. Looking at the outside is what men do and that's what leads them into sin, looking with eyes of spite, envy and violence, getting angry and then when their 'countenances fall' doing worse things. Like Jez did. Love for God and neighbour is what God requires, and that is *only* fully possible through Christ. And *in* Christ. Jesus said we should have faith in Him in our hearts, and love one another too. And you'll then offer that cup of water or bit of help to a neighbour," said Josh. "Both parts. They're both inseparable you see."

"I suppose it all goes wrong in the world," said Seef, "because people envy and want what others have. Some socialist governments try to even things out by calling those who have got, 'oppressors', and those who haven't got, the 'oppressed' - but anyone can see it's not like that, and it never seems to work out with their PC philosophies anyway – there's always our individual wayward hearts that need to repent. Ha-ha! Back in England some would say this wasn't a socially fair arrangement here, that Jezzy is to live in a shed while I or her neighbours are in mansions, or that Mrs Welch is actually *serving* me at home!"

"This is not a place of socialism and democracy, Seef! It is a place of rewards for those who qualify – to enjoy them. Abba Father the King must have their hearts first. They can progress from there, you know. Meantime I must do my work under the 'King of Hearts' as the 'Jack of Hearts' while the world still turns. I'll 'occupy'! Lots to do! I will be getting back to England soon – after lunch with you. There's a Bible study tomorrow, you know, in King's Sternton!"

A few weeks later, Seef looked out from his window and saw Jezzy standing around in his front garden, as if reluctant to come in. She looked so changed. Seef went out and found her in tears.

"Welcome," he said. "Josh said you *had* forgiven me," she cried out to him, "but how can you ever *really* forgive me?" Seef hardly recognised her humble, tearful face. Gone was the arrogance and disdain.

"I can and do forgive you," said Seef. "I've done many things wrong myself, you see. I've *thought* hatred, which you know, according to Jesus, is as bad as actual murder."

Jezzy looked up at him and smiled for the first time. He had never seen her smile like that. In it Seef saw the smile of the little girl many years before who had loved gardening.

"Come in," he said, "I'll show you the shed that we've just put up. You're *very* welcome here."

"And Josh told me, you know, that you have agreed to let me do some work here and tend the garden. That is my heart's desire, and I will be so fulfilled if I do it well. And then after that, he said - I would be able to visit your parents with you, and make a clean breast of it with your dear father."

"He said *that* did he?" exclaimed Seef. "Well this place and Josh himself are becoming more surprising and amazing every day, I must say."

"I've heard so much already that has amazed *me*," said Jezzy. "I've heard we eventually get to go to the mountain country from here, where there is the King, and where there are even more impressive mansions, and that Josh has a wonderful place up there too."

"And *I* get to see my dear old dad – and mum – again. I feel like bursting with happiness. I had a dream on the plane here about it, you know!"

"Well, I reckon this is the place where dreams come true," said Jezzy. "Now, young man, are you going to tell me about your favourite plants and trees for the proposed garden? I would love to start – if that's okay with you of course."

Seef laughed. "Come to the library," he said. "I believe I have a book there all about it!"

The End

Appendix 1

Part of The Book of Jasher, Chapter 1

11 And Adam and his wife transgressed the command of God which he commanded them, and God knew it, and his anger was kindled against them and he cursed them.

12 And the Lord God drove them that day from the Garden of Eden, to till the ground from which they were taken, and they went and dwelt at the east of the Garden of Eden; and Adam knew his wife Eve and she bore two sons and three daughters.

13 And she called the name of the first born Cain, saying, I have obtained a man from the Lord, and the name of the other she called Abel, for she said, In vanity we came into the earth, and in vanity we shall be taken from it.

14 And the boys grew up and their father gave them a possession in the land; and *Cain was a tiller of the ground, and Abel a keeper of sheep.*

15 And it was at the expiration of a few years, that they brought an approximating offering to the Lord, and Cain brought from the fruit of the ground, and Abel brought from the firstlings of his flock from the fat thereof, and God turned and inclined to Abel and his offering, and a fire came down from the Lord from heaven and consumed it.

16 And unto Cain and his offering the Lord did not turn, and he did not incline to it, for he had brought from the

inferior fruit of the ground before the Lord, and Cain was jealous against his brother Abel on account of this, and he sought a pretext to slay him.

17 And in some time after, Cain and Abel his brother, went one day into the field to do their work; and they were both in the field, Cain tilling and ploughing his ground, and Abel feeding his flock; and *the flock passed that part which Cain had ploughed in the ground, and it sorely grieved Cain on this account.*

18 And Cain approached his brother Abel in anger, and he said unto him, What is there between me and thee, that thou comest to dwell and bring thy flock to feed in my land?

19 And Abel answered his brother Cain and said unto him, What is there between me and thee, that thou shalt eat the flesh of my flock and clothe thyself with their wool?

20 And now therefore, put off the wool of my sheep with which thou hast clothed thyself, and recompense me for their fruit and flesh which thou hast eaten, and when thou shalt have done this, I will then go from thy land as thou hast said?

21 And Cain said to his brother Abel, Surely if I slay thee this day, who will require thy blood from me?

22 And Abel answered Cain, saying, Surely God who has made us in the earth, he will avenge my cause, and he will require my blood from thee shouldst thou slay me, for the Lord is the judge and arbiter, and it is he who will requite man according to his evil, and the wicked

man according to the wickedness that he may do upon earth.

23 And now, if thou shouldst slay me here, surely God knoweth thy secret views, and will judge thee for the evil which thou didst declare to do unto me this day.

24 And when Cain heard the words which Abel his brother had spoken, behold the anger of Cain was kindled against his brother Abel for declaring this thing.

25 And *Cain hastened and rose up, and took the iron part of his ploughing instrument, with which he suddenly smote his brother and he slew him,* and Cain spilt the blood of his brother Abel upon the earth, and the blood of Abel streamed upon the earth before the flock.

26 And after this *Cain repented having slain his brother, and he was sadly grieved, and he wept over him and it vexed him exceedingly.*

27 And Cain rose up and dug a hole in the field, wherein he put his brother's body, and he turned the dust over it.

28 And the Lord knew what Cain had done to his brother, and the Lord appeared to Cain and said unto him, Where is Abel thy brother that was with thee?

29 And Cain dissembled, and said, I do not know, am I my brother's keeper? And the Lord said unto him, What hast thou done? *The voice of thy brother's blood crieth unto me from the ground where thou hast slain him.*

30 For thou hast slain thy brother and hast dissembled before me, and didst imagine in thy heart that I saw thee not, nor knew all thy actions.

31 But thou didst this thing and didst slay thy brother for naught and because he spoke rightly to thee, and now, therefore, cursed be thou from the ground which opened its mouth to receive thy brother's blood from thy hand, and wherein thou didst bury him.

32 And it shall be when thou shalt till it, it shall no more give thee its strength as in the beginning, for thorns and thistles shall the ground produce, and thou shalt be moving and wandering in the earth until the day of thy death.

33 And at that time *Cain went out from the presence of the Lord, from the place where he was, and he went moving and wandering* in the land toward the east of Eden, he and all belonging to him.

Appendix 2

Part of Genesis, Chapter 4

1 And Adam knew Eve his wife; and she conceived, and bare Cain, and said, I have gotten a man from the LORD.

2 And she again bare his brother Abel. *And Abel was a keeper of sheep, but Cain was a tiller of the ground.*

3 And in process of time it came to pass, that Cain brought of the fruit of the ground an offering unto the LORD.

4 And Abel, he also brought of the firstlings of his flock and of the fat thereof. And the LORD had respect unto Abel and to his offering:

5 But unto Cain and to his offering he had not respect. And Cain was very wroth, and his countenance fell.

6 And the LORD said unto Cain, *Why art thou wroth? And why is thy countenance fallen?*

7 *If thou doest well, shalt thou not be accepted? And if thou doest not well, sin lieth at the door.* And unto thee shall be his desire, and thou shalt rule over him.

8 And Cain talked with Abel his brother: and it came to pass, when they were in the field, that *Cain rose up against Abel his brother, and slew him.*

9 And the LORD said unto Cain, Where is Abel thy brother? And he said, I know not: Am I my brother's keeper?

10 And he said, What hast thou done? *The voice of thy brother's blood crieth unto me from the ground.*

11 And now art thou cursed from the earth, which hath opened her mouth to receive thy brother's blood from thy hand;

12 When thou tillest the ground, it shall not henceforth yield unto thee her strength; a fugitive and a vagabond shalt thou be in the earth.

13 And Cain said unto the LORD, My punishment is greater than I can bear.

14 Behold, thou hast driven me out this day from the face of the earth; and from thy face shall I be hid; and I shall be a fugitive and a vagabond in the earth; and it shall come to pass, that every one that findeth me shall slay me.

15 And the LORD said unto him, Therefore whosoever slayeth Cain, vengeance shall be taken on him sevenfold. And the LORD set a mark upon Cain, lest any finding him should kill him.

16 And Cain went out from the presence of the LORD, and dwelt in the land of Nod, on the east of Eden.

Printed in Poland
by Amazon Fulfillment
Poland Sp. z o.o., Wrocław

53298762R00103